To the Left of Death

Susan Quilty

First printing, 2018

Cover Design: Susan Quilty
Publisher: Bitter Lily Books, LLC

Library of Congress Control Number: 2021922344
ISBN: 978-1-7379702-2-4
ISBN: 978-1-7379702-3-1

Second Edition, 2022

Bitter Lily Books, LLC
Ashburn, Virginia

SusanQuilty.com

You are
stronger than
you think

Day One

Not many people expect their day to include murder. Homicide detectives. Medical examiners. Judges or criminal lawyers. I guess hitmen and serial killers, too. But not most people. Not the ones who shy away from death. Not even those of us who already know its shadow.

There's a finality to death. However it happens. Whether it comes as a welcome release, a choice, or an unexpected tragedy. There's no second chance. There's no coming back. That's hard for those left behind to accept. Even harder to accept after murder. At least in my experience.

Murder hadn't crossed my mind that morning. Not once. Or not that I remember. To be honest, I don't know what I was thinking that morning. But I wasn't thinking about murder. Looking back—*recreating*—I was probably thinking about clouds.

It had been dark that week. Cold and damp. Everyone had been talking about the rain. Worrying over it, as if it were important. Or maybe just making conversation. Like people do. Finding common ground in the mundane.

I worry more about the climate in my own head. There are winds in there that can churn their way into a hurricane, leaving me stuck in the eye of the storm where it's dark and quiet as gusts swirl just out of reach. When that storm kicks up, the other people in my life—friends, acquaintances, a husband—all exist on the other side. Separated. Distant.

I try not see the storm. To not let it take me away.

That morning, the bed was empty. George had stumbled downstairs before I woke up. He uses the automatic setting to have his coffee waiting first thing, like clockwork. It's a very normal way to start the day. He drinks his coffee in front of the news, hits the treadmill or goes outside for a thirty-minute run, then heads back upstairs for his shower just as I'm leaving for work.

It's his routine. A normal routine for a normal man.

Sometimes when I think about George's normalcy, his discipline and easy manner, I feel small and brittle. Fragile. Yet somehow soft and oozing, too. Seeping into the cracks of other people's schedules. Other people's plans.

Sometimes I marvel at being married to a man named George. It's such a grown-up, sensible name. Not a husband name I would have daydreamed about in junior high. Not a Dominic or Tristan or Shane.

Sometimes I marvel at being married at all.

I had my own morning routine by then. Each weekday began with a vintage-style dress, a coordinating cardigan, and ballet flats. A uniform of sorts. An outfit that felt nothing like the real me, but entirely like my teacher persona. I'd tell myself the look was ironic, a quiet rebellion. I might not have planned on being a teacher, I'd tell myself, but I could have fun with it. With dressing up and playing the part.

When it came time to choose a grade, I'd thought third wouldn't be so bad. An age when kids were firmly rooted as kids. The baby years left behind but not yet teetering on the verge of teenage angst. Not yet struggling against real problems.

It didn't take long to realize that I'd been wrong.

That morning, I wore a white dress with a blue floral print, a blue sweater, and white flats. Something was missing, so I added a thin, red belt for that pop of color. It was the kind of kicky detail fashion magazines might recommend. If I ever read them. Or if I were the kind of person to use words like *kicky* without irony.

It's easy to recreate that moment in my mind. To imagine pulling that dress from the closet and unfolding that sweater. I can still feel the material when I close my eyes. The softness of the cotton, the thick plastic of the buttons. The stiff vinyl belt that wouldn't be the only red on my dress by the end of the day.

I picture myself that morning and think that was the day that changed me—that irrevocably set me apart from everyone else—but that may not be entirely true.

Even before that day, I knew I was different.

When I wasn't at school teaching, or at home grading papers, I was dropping ecstasy at an underground rave. I was draped in neon clothing and light-up jewelry that was so out, it was in. I was dancing in a throng of sweaty bodies and feeling a crush of flesh blotting out the impending storm.

Except I was never actually there. Not at the rave or anywhere else. I was really at home, in front of the TV, curled up on the couch and eating ice cream while George dozed beside me. But I was only partially watching the show. The rest of my mind was at that rave, or bungee jumping off an iron bridge, or standing on the upper wall of an abandoned parking deck, or racing 100 miles an hour on the back of a motorcycle. I was lost in the past or in my own imagination. I was anywhere but sitting on that couch where I was dying day-by-day and slowly getting fat.

Other people feel the same way—they must—but those people were hidden in my suburban life. Or maybe hidden in plain sight. Either way, I didn't see them.

The people I knew talked about TV and movies, parenting and bills. Some would rant about sports, and most would joke about not having time to finish a book. They seemed content beneath their complaints and middle-class exhaustion. They seemed to be getting enough out of life or were resigned to getting as much as they were.

They weren't the teenage outcasts I'd left in my ancient past or the dark-and-twisty friends I'd planned to make in New York.

Still, I imagine they had their own personal storms. Demons, ghosts, issues. So many euphemisms for personal pain. It's an unspoken misery for most people, but I would catch a glimpse of it from time to time. Pick up clues that others were struggling, too. Coping in their own way. There's a kinship that springs up occasionally. As if people naturally gravitate toward those who are equally broken.

Underneath. But that wasn't discussed. Not directly. Not in the suburbs where life revolved around soccer games and work commutes.

It could hurt to feel broken in that kind of setting. To feel so out of place.

Though it was easier when I was drinking.

There's something soothing about holding a wine glass, a rocks glass, or even a beer bottle in a pinch. Something safe and happy. It's like a modern-day shield. Stemmed glasses are best, cradled in the hand and carried through-out gestures, like cigarettes were once used to punctuate conversations. And are still used, in some circles, where the notion of healthy lungs hasn't quite caught up to the vices of daily survival.

Alcohol is more widely accepted than cigarettes in my circle. It functions as a common way to pass an evening. Or an afternoon. It breaks down barriers and draws people together in a self-medicated haze.

§

I didn't see George at all that morning. The sky had cleared, and he'd gone outside for his run. I didn't think much of it at the time, and it isn't all that important now. Except that I wonder about it when I recreate that morning. I imagine where he might have been when I was getting into my car and driving away. He may have been just around the corner or several blocks away. Sometimes I'd see him just as I was leaving.

Sometimes I miss him.

At school, once the kids had arrived and the bell had rung, I'd noticed Mindy's absence. Again. Three days in a row. She'd been missing too often and the bruises on her small arms and legs had bothered me a lot more than they worried the social worker who was keeping an eye on her home life. They were probably nothing, I'd been told. Kids get bumps and bruises. There was no cause for alarm yet. But they'd keep tabs a little longer, just to be sure.

The *yets* and *probablys* had made my stomach twitch at another absence. It's those doubts that leave you open to bad ideas.

I'd met Mindy's dad by then. Twice. He'd barely said a word to me. About his daughter or anything else. He'd shown up at Back to School Night, sat quietly at her little desk and left the moment I'd finished my speech. He wasn't rude about leaving, and he wasn't even the first to go. But he also wasn't one of the parents who'd lingered to ask questions, or give me specific instructions, or offer helpful suggestions. At our first and only conference—the one I'd called to test out the situation—he'd listened to what I'd had to say, then nodded and thanked me without sharing anything substantial of his own.

I try to recreate details from that meeting. Any detail that might give me answers about Ed Dombrowski. About the person he'd been before he'd died bleeding in my arms. But it's hard to get insight from *hellos* and *goodbyes*.

Every expression that had passed over his face is now open to endless interpretation. At the time, I'd been struck by his sadness. Or that's how I remember it now.

I wasn't the one who had contacted Social Services about Mindy. Liz had done that the previous spring, after a car accident had killed Mindy's mother. After Mindy's dark drawings and small injuries had made Liz suspicious. She'd fretted over Mindy and worried about her father, claiming he wouldn't work with her, wouldn't open up to her. Claiming he hadn't been completely sober since the day his wife had died.

The whole story had been laid out for me as soon as Mindy was assigned to my class. Mostly by Liz and partly by the case worker who'd followed up on Mindy's progress. None of the story came to me from Mindy. Or from Ed himself. Not until the day he died, and those moments hadn't told me much.

After he died, the idea of Ed haunted me more than his actual memory. Though the memories were bad, too. The sight, the smell, the feel.

I'd think about Ed when I was drinking. Usually when drinking alone. Or I'd drink when thinking about Ed. It's hard to know which came first.

They call it self-medicating. The drinking alone. To me, it was a fortification against the storm. I sometimes wonder what Ed had called it. If he'd called it anything at all. I wonder if he'd had a storm in his head or if it was more of a void. I wonder what it had been like for him to be left behind.

Whatever he'd called it, he'd been doing it that day. There was a bottle of scotch on his coffee table and a glass in his hand when Liz and I showed up at his door. I'd smelled it on him right away—oaky with a hint of peat—and had been annoyed with myself for liking the scent. Even now, in the recreation, the scotch smells warm and gentle.

There had been nothing Liz liked about the scotch. She'd taken one look at his glass and pushed her way in, spewing accusations and calling out Mindy's name. It happened fast after that. Faster than my brain can untangle. The shouting, the shove, the gun shot. The blood on my hands as I felt for a pulse at his lifeless neck.

§

In the days after Ed's death, George made an effort to talk. He wanted to hear the story and know how I felt. He wanted me to see a counselor, but I'd had enough of that. He wanted me to cry, I think, and I did. I couldn't help but cry in those first few days, and weeks, when Ed's body—his blood—appeared every time I closed my eyes. George poured me drinks, but never scotch, and held me on the couch.

I cried more than I talked, and that helped. In practical ways. No one asked much once the tears began to flow. Half-sentences and brief answers were enough, even for Detective Frye and the lawyer George had hired. It was an open-and-shut case, and it wasn't shutting on me. I wasn't the guilty one. Not legally. I was the one who had called 911. I was the one who had begged Ed to live and had held my blue sweater against his steady stream of blood.

And through it all, the storm had raged on. It had whipped to hurricane force, blotting out the passing of time and leaving me with snapshot moments to file and tuck aside in a way that would do the least harm.

I wonder if it'd been like that for Liz. Or for Mindy.

§

I wondered about Liz and Mindy a lot for the first year or so. I knew where they were, but I didn't see them. One visit to Liz was enough for us both, and more than enough for the orderlies who'd had to restrain her. Seeing her that way had made the earlier Liz seem like an illusion or an imaginary friend. I'd known there was a reason she'd been so passionate about helping kids, even if she'd never told me herself. It was the kind of thing I could sense. Equally broken people. Except Liz had been more broken than she'd let on. Or I'm more broken than I realize and haven't yet taken to carrying a gun.

There's no reliable way to tell which is true.

I put Liz out of my mind after that visit. Would I have done that if I'd known then what I know now? Maybe not. Or maybe she was more than I could manage.

Mindy went to live with an aunt and uncle. Her mother's sister. I was told they were happy to have her.

I often wondered if Mindy would show up someday. Grown-up and asking for answers. That's why I'd sift through the memories and recreate the details. I'd wanted to give grown-up Mindy honest answers when she asked about the day her father was murdered. The day he was shot dead while she lay sick and feverish beside the bowl of chicken noodle soup that he'd just brought her.

She may not remember much of that day herself. She might remember the raised voices. Maybe the crack of the gunshot and Liz storming into her room. I can't help her with that piece of the puzzle though, if she were to ask. I wasn't there. I'd stayed behind with her dying father.

They'd asked me why I'd gone to Ed in that moment. Instead of chasing down Liz, who, for all I knew, was still wielding a gun. I didn't have a good answer, except to honestly say that the idea of Liz hurting Mindy had never crossed my mind. A man had been shot and I hadn't thought about what to do next.

Not that I remember.

The neighbors had called 911, too, which was good because I may not have said anything useful on my call. I remember saying, *"He's been shot. Send help."* And something about all the blood. Or maybe I only remember that being played back by the police. I think the 911 operator asked me where the shooter was and if I was in danger, but my brain was focused on the flow of blood and on anything I could do to make it stop.

When the police arrived, the front door was standing open, and Ed was dead. But I didn't know that.

Or I didn't *want* to know that.

I had my sweater pressed against his chest and I kept calling for help, yelling that I couldn't find his pulse.

Liz was in the bedroom by then, rocking Mindy in her arms but calling her Karly—the name of her own long-dead little sister. I didn't know that until much later. Maybe days later? I didn't know Liz had dropped her gun on the hallway floor either, but I did know she wasn't there to hurt Mindy. No one had to tell me that. I just knew.

My role wasn't apparent in those first few moments. Not to the police. But my compliance made it easy for them to lead me out of the house. To stand me by a police car and ask me questions. Later, they said—someone said—that I'd been in shock. They said that was why I walked in a daze and didn't remember to ask about Mindy until I was out in the fresh air.

If a grown-up Mindy ever visits me, it might not be easy to explain why I didn't run in to protect her or even worry about her safety. But at least I'd tried to save her dad's life. Even if I was the one who'd brought his murderer to their home.

Day Two

Mindy and Liz never went back to our school, but I did. After I was investigated, evaluated, and cleared. I went back the following fall. Mainly because I didn't know what else to do.

The new guidance counselor was cautious around me, offering help he didn't really want to give. The rest of the staff divided along a thin line of judgment and defense. Some thought I was as much to blame because I'd driven Liz to the house. Others said I couldn't have known what Liz was going to do.

My personal truth, carried so deep I could barely see it, fell somewhere in between. It would shift toward one side or the other, teetering between guilt and innocence, unsettled by my shadowy memories. But I kept that to myself.

In those early days, I fell back into the safety of my usual habits. The routine was important then. The going through the motions. It was comforting to make myself go on as if nothing had changed. As if I could withstand anything and never really lose the core of me.

People like to think that way. That they are the same person before and after a trauma, just wiser and stronger for the experience. They talk about being different, for sure, but in the sense of having a new perspective. I think it's different than that. Deeper than that. I think some events go beyond giving you a wiser point of view. Some memories—some thoughts—seep in, even after the scarring of the tragedy itself, and they continue to eat away at the person you once were. Those thoughts—those unrelenting recreations—twist and shape you until you become someone else. Someone you don't entirely recognize.

Or maybe those relentless thoughts just bring out the things you'd wanted to hide. Cracks under the surface stretching too wide to be bridged by social pretense.

It's going on four years since Ed's blood covered my hands, and there are times when I'm genuinely surprised to see that my hands are clean. The realization comes in a split-second moment, as a shock and a nauseous dread. As if I've lost the blood and need to get it back.

The blood itched that day, as it began to dry and cake against my skin. It flaked off me when I moved, on the way to the hospital and before they cleaned me up. I watched tiny bits fall to the ground and felt a panicked desire to gather them up. I didn't want to let them go. I wasn't ready to stop fighting. If I could just stuff every fleck of dried blood back inside Ed's body, where they belonged, he might still have a chance. He was healthy before the gunshot, before the blood had poured out, and he needed his blood to be healthy again.

I may have been in shock, but there's a primitive logic in that thought that still trips me up. A visceral dread in knowing that his precious blood had been flaked off and washed away. And in the knowing that I'd let it go.

§

Since that day, everyone else has gotten back to normal. George, the other teachers, our friends. I met with my book club each month and the shooting stopped coming up. It was a relief at first, but after a while I wondered why they'd lost interest.

They'd talk about a girl growing up on a horse farm, a boy adrift at sea, a man remembering his days in the circus, but not about reality. They let those imaginary stories be a distraction. A misdirection from the terrible world we live in as we laugh and talk, and drink our wine, and quietly hope we won't be the next victim in the national news.

And it isn't fair to think any of that. Because they'd tried to be there for me. The way people do when there's nothing else they can offer. They'd wanted to listen—and still would—if I'd just open my mouth and let them in. But what could I say?

It was easier to sit back and listen. To be there and not be there. Until the day when something finally caught my attention. It was at a book club meeting when Annemarie cut through my clouded thoughts by saying, "Anyone who has an affair could not possibly love their spouse."

The other women nodded thoughtfully, shrugged uncertainly, or glanced around to gauge each other's reactions. They were moving in slow motion, exaggerated and unreal, the way people do when there are too many of them in one place.

"Books like this just make excuses for immature people who can't control their hormones."

"That's awfully harsh," Holly countered, as expected. They've adopted those roles in our group. Annemarie with her conservative pronouncements and Holly with her liberal, to-each-their-own mentality, leaving the rest of us to join in with varying degrees of outrage or support.

"Now you're defending cheating husbands?"

Sarcastic questions excite Annemarie, even as she frowns to soften the glint in her eye. They raise tension in the room, creating an urgency to take sides and win the fight. It's an echo of high school drama that we're too mature to acknowledge and too human to ignore.

Holly doesn't enjoy those debates as much, but she's compelled to show the other side. To not let us fall too far into the suburban complacency of our upper middle-class existence. She doesn't enjoy Annemarie either. As a person. When Holly talks to Annemarie, she reminds me of a family dog putting up with a toddler pulling its ears.

Holly frowned and we waited to see how she would frame the flip side. Instead, she shook her head, maybe wishing she hadn't said anything at all. "Well, no, not exactly… But it can be complicated. Sometimes people who cheat deserve more sympathy than anger."

"Sympathy!" Annemarie wasn't the type to give anyone an out. "You're going to sit here and say you'd forgive your husband if he cheated on you? You'd actually believe that he still loved you?"

Holly hesitated, uncharacteristically quiet. Her fingers were twining and untwining, her head bowed low. The room stretched and contracted around her, bringing heat that prickled my lungs.

"I would."

It took a moment to realize that the words had come out of my mouth. Not Holly's.

"Really?" Annemarie turned her sarcasm my way and the others froze. They may not talk about the shooting anymore, but there's a difference in the way they treat me now. A caution. I'm fragile now, with one more trauma than a person should have. Or maybe more than one.

"I could believe he still loved me."

That distinction was important to me. Forgiveness was more complicated.

"If you *love* someone," Annemarie responded condescendingly, "their feelings come before your own selfish desires. No one cheats on someone and still loves them."

"Maybe love isn't that simple." I was feeling my way through the words, catching pace with a room that moved out of sync with my reality. First too fast, then too slow. Time expanding to let all eyes turn my way but not long enough to settle my mind into any coherent thought beyond the certainty that nothing is that black and white.

"*Real* love is that simple," Annemarie insisted. "It's as simple as right and wrong, not this romance novel version of infatuation and lust, and... and cosmic meant-to-be."

"This isn't a *romance* novel!" Emily's quick defense of her book choice opened the floodgates. Everyone spoke at once then, stumbling over each other to dissect the characters and their extenuating circumstances.

My brain made a lazy attempt to pick up snatches of the conversation before giving up and focusing my hands on pouring another glass of wine. Through the gesticulating blur, I saw Holly sitting across the room. She sipped her wine quietly, as if listening intently, but she was no longer participating. Her eyes drifted toward me in a far-off way, watching me or just gazing in my direction, but making no attempt to communicate. At least, not that I could see.

At the end of the night, Holly asked me for a ride home. She'd walked over from the next block, when it was light, but didn't want to brave the dark alone. It was a normal enough request as the group broke apart, each of us making sure the others had a secure path home. Hoping for safety in numbers. There was small-talk on the short drive and quiet as I pulled up to the curb in front of her house. A sense of anticipation had crept into the hum of the engine. The car parked ahead of us was bright red but looked deep orange in the glare of my headlights.

In the darkness, Holly said, "I cheated on Joe."

Her voice was flat. Her tone was dull. But there was a quiver in the sigh that followed.

Sometimes news like that comes as a shock, other times it materializes with a little click of recognition. Like finding a piece that fills out the puzzle of a person just a little bit more. It comes as a comfort, in a way. A step toward turning a paper doll acquaintance into a fellow survivalist. Someone just trying to weather their own life. And not always getting it right.

I nodded in acceptance but took a moment to gather my thoughts. It wasn't clear what she needed me to say.

"Do you think I'm a terrible person?"

"Not at all."

"It was a long time ago. Before we had Kelly. Back in that first year we were married, when we were getting used to living together and it was all just so much harder than I thought it should be. You know?"

"Yeah."

I knew.

"It was like, I had this idea of what marriage would be like before the wedding, but then nothing lived up to it. I just kept thinking, *'It shouldn't be this hard.'* And then Joe took that damn consulting job where he was across the country four days a week, and it was like he was running away because he knew it was too hard, too."

Once she started, the story poured out in those words. Or words like them. I slipped the car into park, letting the engine idle, and eased my foot off the gas pedal. The radio was on low, playing a too-cheery commercial, but reaching to turn it off might have broken whatever spell had given Holly the courage to talk. I heard her out and nodded along. Being *there for her.*

"I still love Joe. I loved him the whole stupid time. Loved them both in a way, because it wasn't so much about… about the affair, as it was a way for me to figure out what I really wanted. About who I really was, as an adult. If that makes any kind of sense?"

"Yes," I agreed.

She wanted more, but the storm was rustling, whispering winds that got in the way of helpful thoughts. I wasn't shocked or upset, and I didn't think less of her. I felt something. But the something was fleeting and unfamiliar. Or maybe distantly familiar, like something I hadn't felt in a very long time.

"People do that," I added at last, skipping over whatever nebulous feeling was forming inside and trying instead to voice a thought I'd had many times before that night. "People lose themselves and find themselves over and over. It's never easy."

Holly nodded and wiped away the tears that had slid down her cheeks.

Part of me wanted to cry with her. Like it might be the polite thing to do. Or the thing I would have done—had done—back when we were younger. And closer. Part of me wanted to physically reach out, but to do what? To hold, to pat, to hug, to touch?

My hands stayed resting in my lap, but my right forearm began to shift, maybe the precursor to a movement I hadn't entirely thought out.

"I can't believe I just blurted all that out!" Holly's awkward laugh shattered the sanctity and left my arm resting in place. Heavy and still.

I looked her way then, feeling like it was somehow okay again. Letting our eyes lock and hold.

"Secret's safe with me," I reassured with our old kind of smile, and Holly nodded with a fresh batch of tears and a quivering laugh.

"I don't know why it feels so good to finally tell someone, but thanks. For listening."

For being there, added a voice in my brain.

Holly left the car and I drove away, expecting to never talk about it again. But something in that shared confidence made me feel flushed and shaky. It was the way our eyes had met for just a moment, looking straight through the quieted storm.

Holly was pregnant when Ed died. Around four or five months. It was past the public announcement but not yet time for the shower. She was starting to show and was fixated on cribs, car seats, strollers, and all the stuff babies need. The necessities. The accessories.

After that day, Holly was rattled. More than most. It was the violence of it, and the finality. But there was something else, too. She was struck by the judgment. By the way Liz had watched Ed from the outside and decided that he was an unfit parent. Not just unfit, but unfit enough that he deserved to die.

Holly knew Liz wasn't well—we all knew it after the story hit the news—but she said that only made it worse. She asked if it was always that way. If deeply damaged people always go unnoticed until they commit a violent crime. She wanted to know if parents could ever really protect their kids from the outside world.

I didn't have any answers to her questions. I was caught up in questions of my own.

Holly wasn't my only pregnant friend back then. It was one of those times. A year when so many decided they were ready to have a first or start fresh with another one. By a certain age, it's biology. But I haven't felt it yet. My mother blames Liz, saying she'd have grandkids by now if I hadn't been traumatized by *that crazy woman*. I respond by pouring another glass of wine.

My mother might be onto something about the trauma, but it's difficult to accept that when she focuses on the shooting and easily forgets the rest. Leaving out my entire life before Liz pulled out a gun.

It's easy for some people to look at a situation from the outside and call it by a certain name, even if that name is wrong. It makes them feel safer. In control. And they almost always make that call with large chunks of missing data. Important chunks from an earlier time or another place. They only remember the parts of the story that fit their current theory. It's confirmation bias, really. They have an idea and that's what it is, whether all the pieces fit or not.

Maybe that's a good thing, for them, because it makes life fit a nice, safe pattern.

My brain doesn't work that way. When I step back and try to observe my own life, it looks more like a yard sale jigsaw: jumbled pieces from a mix of puzzles but not enough—or too many—to fit into a solid picture.

Holly was happy again in time for her baby shower. She laughed while opening gifts and showing off the baby's freshly painted nursery. I knew she hadn't found any actual answers, but her questions had faded into the background.

Maybe that's what you have to do to be a parent. Bury the fear and tell yourself that nothing like that will happen to you or to your family.

It was good she found some peace, but I didn't know how she did it. Not when the questions in my head had only gotten louder. I was a ghost at her shower. There and not there but glad to have someone else be the focus. At a baby shower, no one wanted to think about death, an orphaned child, or the insanity of a murderer. I represented those sordid things and was left to ponder my questions alone. Which was a relief. Mostly.

I found ways to stay away while nominally taking part. It was easy to do and barely noticed. Adult friendships are like that. Everyone busy and their lives only intersecting in the odd moments of overlapping free time.

Not having kids made it easier to stay on the fringes. There were no regular play dates or carpooling schedules. I could drop in for book club, birthdays, and random events, then fade back into the shadows.

There were breakthrough moments, like that night in my car with Holly. Moments that felt like a door creaking open and an opportunity to connect. But I didn't know how to step over the threshold. And did I really want to?

Do I want to now?

In the years since our friends' baby boom, I didn't know that George was in their camp. I didn't know there were baby urges hiding in his stoic repetition of the day-to-day. He was patiently waiting, and I was ignorant of the signs. Or I wasn't paying attention.

It feels odd to have not known for so long, the way discovered truth often does. It should have become obvious at some point, living together every day.

When it finally came out, I wanted to believe that I had known on some level all along. But I hadn't. And that was the scary part. The wondering what else I didn't know about him and realizing that he didn't know me either.

The truth came out on a rainy Sunday. I was reading at the kitchen island while George sorted the junk mail and random papers that had a way of reappearing despite my efforts at keeping the clutter in check.

"This is today?"

He waved a pastel card in my direction. I'd already told Beth we couldn't make her three-year-old's party, and I'd meant to throw the card away.

I shrugged a yes, confident in his ability to read the date on the invitation.

"And we're not going?"

He sounded upset, and I looked up from my book.

"Did you want to?"

"It's a little late to ask now."

George dropped the card in the trash and pulled open the fridge, scanning the contents before fishing out a bottle of water. When he didn't say more, I stopped watching him, but I couldn't read the next paragraph in my book. My eyes passed over the words without taking them in. It was an unsettling sensation, but before I could try a third time, George's sarcasm cut in.

"It would have been nice to be asked."

He began pacing then, twisting the cap of his water bottle on and off.

"I'm sorry."

I didn't like his tense pacing, but there wasn't anything else to say. I turned back to the book, still concerned that my brain had forgotten how to interpret written words, and I felt a rising panic. There was an awareness that something I'd done had upset George and a confusion in not entirely knowing what. I stopped trying to read the book.

As the minutes steadily ticked away, it became harder to know what to do or say.

"You really don't give a shit about how I feel, do you?"

His outburst was cold water in my face. A punch in the gut. All those clichés that leave you startled and flushed, cold and shaky, and unsure how to proceed.

I should've put the book down then, but I didn't. It felt safer to stay very still and speak very calmly. With my eyes on the blurry page, I said the first words that came to mind.

"I never said that."

And he slammed the water bottle on the counter.

George was out of patience, shaking his head in tiny jerks and half-chuckling in an angry, ugly way. And then he was farther away. Shifting in space. Or I was shifting. Slipping away to a place where no one could find me. A place inside the storm where the winds were loud but not touching me directly. More shield than prison.

"You don't have to *say* it," George shot back bitterly, but the words were hazy and hard to hear. If he said more, I didn't catch it. The room was very large then as I pulled in, withdrawing to a shadowy hideaway that was large and dim and muffled. I was lost in thoughts that were nothing but a jumble of unconnected words. Bits of song lyrics, clichéd phrases, lines from movies, the name of my third-grade teacher. None of it was relevant or even completely heard. It was whispered and buzzed. Too fast. Too loud. Too quiet. I forgot I was holding the book, open in both hands, until George came across the room, gently taking it away and setting it on the island.

He held my hands in both of his. His breathing had slowed, and his body was still. I became aware that time had passed and the winds were dying down. My muscles were rigid, tight, and sore. There was a dull ache spreading across my head. George was patient again. Silently calling me back from the shadowy place and waiting as I glanced around the kitchen, bright and cozy and safe. As safe as it had ever been.

We didn't talk about the storm that swirled between us or my losing minutes in its wake. I'd told him once, years ago, but his look of pity had made me wish I'd stayed quiet. I wanted to pull my hands away. Laugh it off. Be normal. Continue on as if I'd never left.

Shifting my eyes, I saw the closed book on the counter.

"I wasn't reading it."

He squeezed my hands reassuringly and smiled.

"I know."

The kitchen was too bright and George was too close. Everything around me was crowding back in but softly. A slow suffocation.

"I'm sorry about the party," I told him carefully. "I didn't think you'd want to go."

He nodded slowly, considering. "You didn't want to go?"

"To a toddler's birthday party?"

"To Beth and Steve's party for their toddler," George clarified, and I wanted to see his point. "We haven't been to their new house yet and it could have been fun."

"With a bunch of sticky kids running around on a sugar high? Aren't there better ways to visit?"

George's sigh told me this talk would go on longer than either of us could maintain our crouched positions. Extricating my hands, I made a careful show of easing my tight muscles. It was the way I might communicate with someone who didn't speak English. Or with a gorilla in the wild. Crossing a vast communication barrier with a simple show of movement. Taking my cue, George straightened up, too. He flexed his fingers and shrugged his shoulders in an exaggerated roll.

The movement took the pressure off, and I wanted the conversation to be over. My bed would be so soft, my covers so warm against the chill of the day. I willed him to simply let it go. But he didn't.

"I thought you liked kids."

It wasn't a question, but there was something reaching in his words. Something sad and wistful that made me consider the idea more carefully. I liked my friends' kids well enough. I liked my kids—my students. But when the invitation had come, with its pink writing and princess border, I'd known that I didn't want to be there.

"Toddlers aren't exactly kids," I said at last, not knowing why this party had made my stomach churn.

"So, no toddlers? No babies?" An edge had crept into George's voice and I knew we were on dangerous ground.

I didn't have any words to add to my shrug.

"I've been waiting for the right time," he said. "To talk about it. But maybe there won't ever be a right time. Maybe this time is as good as any."

I don't remember if I said anything then. I think I only stared as a prickling sensation spread up from my chest and inched its way along my jaw. It's hard to remember anything but his next words.

"We never talk about starting a family."

The sadness in his voice changed the course of the conversation. It wasn't about babies or kids. It was about George then, and the hurt in his eyes. It was about realizing I had missed this important need. And I didn't want to believe that I had missed it so completely.

"It comes up."

"When?"

"Every time your mother visits."

He sighed and spread his hands on the counter. I sifted through my memories of those conversations.

"You always shut her down," I added, as if that made my case.

"That's not us talking about it."

He was right. But I sat silently, letting my non-answer speak for me because I knew what question was coming next. The direct question that would need a direct answer.

I felt his eyes on me and he didn't seem angry anymore. Just sad. Or maybe disappointed.

"You used to want kids," he said. Instead of asking the question.

"Did I?"

It wasn't something I ever remembered wanting, but George was nodding already.

"Back in college," he said wistfully. "We'd sit around planning the future. Two kids. A girl, then a boy. You wanted to name them after our grandparents, to give them roots. You don't remember?"

When he looked up, his smile was dazzling. It was still sad but tinged with the promise of young dreams.

And this time the shock was less acute. There was no punch in the gut or splash of cold water. This time it snuck up on me as a gradual realization. As an idea that I couldn't escape once it had taken shape in my mind. Yet the hurt of it was so much worse that tears burned in the corners of my eyes.

"That wasn't me," I told him as kindly as I could. "You're remembering Jessica."

Day Four

The realization shocked George. I saw it in the way his eyes crinkled, shifted, narrowed, and, at last, widened in horror. I heard it in the hoarse tone of his apology. In his stream of *damns* and *oh-fucks*. His hands trembled when they pulled me close, but I couldn't take the shock away. I could only reassure him with pretty lies. It was okay. It didn't mean anything. It was understandable and he was only human. I said he hadn't meant to hurt me, and that was true, even if it still hurt.

That night, after George was asleep, I poured myself a makeshift Manhattan. No measuring, just everything eyed and swirled together in a rocks glass with one small piece of ice and three extra cherries. There was too much vermouth, but that was easy to fix by adding another shot of bourbon. As I poured, I watched the liquid creep up the sides of the glass. The cherries were nestled in the bottom, still round and smooth, but they would swell over time, filling with alcohol until they cracked under the pressure. Such an obvious parallel it bordered on the absurd.

Wandering around the house at night, glass in hand, the rooms lost their daytime shapes but picked up new details in the bluish light. The TV refelcted the streetlight outside. A white blanket floated against the dark couch. And all around the house creaked with small sounds normally swallowed up by our daytime routine.

In the moonlit den, bookshelves added subtle texture to the walls, and the recliner was a dark mass in the far corner. I perched on the edge of its leather seat, letting my eyes adjust to the dim light, and wondered if anyone else was awake. Holly or Emily or Beth. A friend I could call, just to talk. Holly was at the top of my list but keeping her secret didn't give me the right to late night phone calls. Besides, she was perpetually busy, balancing parenthood with her suburban-friendly side-business of baking custom cakes for special events. Her downtime was all frosting and laundry, and our attempts at plans never went beyond hopefully saying, "let's get coffee sometime!"

Back in high school, late night calls were the norm. Hours of talking about nothing. Thinking out loud with human sounding boards who were just as lost and confused. College was meeting in person. Late nights at diners or bars. Cigarettes and coffee and alcohol. Loud music and the drone of conversations all around. There were pranks and dates and bad decisions. And there was George, picking up the pieces of my self-destruction and rescuing me from the worst in myself.

A stack of notebooks caught my eye. They'd been stashed and forgotten on a lower bookshelf, but I knew them. They were mostly blank. My abandoned attempts at journaling. They stretched across the years. Tiny islands of words captured amid a sea of empty pages. Attempts at getting the loudest thoughts out of my head.

I pulled a book from the stack at random. It was thick and spiral-bound, and I knew before turning on the small reading light that it wasn't one of my journals after all.

It was a sketchpad, and I was afraid to open it.

I took another sip of my drink as the book sat closed on my lap. It was waiting. Taunting. I had to open it, once I'd found it, but it took a moment of preparation. A moment to brace and pull myself together. I slid my fingers under the pale blue cover to feel the thick paper within. Soft and cotton-like. Slightly textured. The book was old and worn, the edges frayed, and the corners bent.

This was a high school sketchpad. Its best drawings had been ripped out for art projects and my hopeful portfolio, leaving these tattered pages behind. There were other books somewhere, better ones from my semester of art school. Probably packed away with my drawing supplies. All those pencils and charcoals in a red shoebox. But this sketchpad had been missed and tucked away between a pile of failed words. If it had been a later book, I might have put it back unopened, but this book had a special pull. What was left, after the best had been taken away?

In the soft light of the reading lamp, forgotten drawings came back to life. There were partial portraits, cartoons, a few smudgy landscapes. My hands itched at the sight of them, fingers tingling as they brushed the cottony pages.

Without a conscious plan, I fished a plain number-two pencil and a soft eraser from the desk, took a large swig of my drink, and curled into the recliner with a blank page open on my lap.

Shapes began to fill the page. Slowly, then more quickly as my confidence returned. There were shaded cubes and trailing vines. Rounded spheres and tight spirals. A lightly sketched almond shape appeared in the lower third of the empty space, followed by a careful circle, an iris, a pupil. I sketched in a soft lid and a line of short, straight lashes. Next, a duplicate appeared, reversed to form a pair. They were sad eyes, but as they looked at me directly, I recognized them. I saw their similarity to a set of sad eyes which had never looked at me so plainly. Eyes that had looked through me. Detached. In despair.

I'd always had a thing for drawing eyes. They showed up in all my doodles eventually, sometimes in pairs and sometimes alone. I'd spent months, years, practicing how to shade them just right. I'd practiced with Jessica when she was too tired to get out of bed. I have a whole set stashed away somewhere. Page after page of her eyes. Each pair slightly different. Some tired, some happy, some scared. But the eyes I'd just drawn were not Jessica's.

They were Ed's.

Turning pages until I found another blank canvas, I drew those eyes again, this time with the distant stare I remembered from our parent-teacher conference. And from that day at his house as well. In the moments before there was blood. I sketched a brow, the bridge of a nose, strong cheekbones, and a square jaw. My thumb and fingers smudged in shading as his features rose from the page, hazy and half-formed. Dirty prints smeared my rocks glass, and I dried my damp fingers on my pajama pants before letting them touch the soft paper again. It was slow going as I moved over his face, adding depth with small details. Faint lines from the nose to the mouth, a careful stubble along the jaw. Small crinkles around the eyes, laugh lines that worked against the sad gaze but still looked right. They showed a man who had once laughed often and the strain of his more recent pain.

His short, rumpled hair was an easy addition, but my memory of it wasn't as clear. Was it this short? Longer? As I whisked in each hair, I pictured Ed's last haircut. When had it been? Its similar length on the three occasions I'd seen him told me it had been cut somewhat regularly. But by whom? By the same person?

"I'm so sorry about your wife." I muttered the words I imagined his regular stylist would say after the accident. But that didn't seem right. He probably went someplace new. A small, cheap place in a strip mall. A place where a different person could cut it each time. Someone who wouldn't expect conversation or who would carry the small talk herself. He would let her prattle on about her day, the weather, her problems, while he waited for this necessary interaction to be done.

"Do you have kids?"

A slight nod. Then adding, "A daughter," because he wouldn't want to be rude.

"My husband wants us to have kids," I chatted lightly, the way the stylist would, while carefully penciling in his sideburns. "But it's not really my thing."

No answer. Or maybe a non-committal *hmm.*

I swallowed the last of my drink, wiped my hand, and studied the picture. Ed's face and hair floated in the center of the page. He needed a neck and the open collar of the blue button-down shirt he was wearing on that last day. My hands moved slowly, imagining the width of his neck, getting it wrong and gradually widening it to a size that matched his disembodied head.

"You're a good father." The words came out without thought, but as I heard them, I knew they were true. "You were struggling, but you were doing your best."

The soft whisk of the pencil filled the room. My thumb smudged lines on instinct, my hands remembering techniques my mind had forgotten. When I saw my glass was empty, I took a quick break, refilling it with plain bourbon to save time. His collar started out too sharp. I erased and redrew, softening the lines of its crumpled, cotton twill.

"George and I talked about having kids tonight," I confessed hesitantly. "Sort of."

His silence was strangely encouraging.

"He brought up a conversation he thought we'd had a long time ago." I didn't want to say the words out loud, but they were there. Still aching. The knowledge that George had confused me with my sister.

I glanced at Ed's eyes, but he was still looking away, slightly through me.

"George was in love with my sister first. Before me." It sounded wrong to say it that way, when there was so much more to the story, but it was the truth. "They met in college. End of her first year and his third." I told him how happy she was that year. How my parents were so sure the remission would last this time. I hadn't been as sure, but that was my way, especially back then. I didn't want to be hopeful and then see the cancer come back again. I used to think that being angry and guarded would make it easier, but it didn't.

Ed's collar took shape as I whispered the story. A placket of buttons marched down the middle of his chest, the top one undone. His shoulders were more difficult for some reason. They wouldn't come out right and the eraser marks from each restart were marring the paper, leaving tell-tale streaks of past mistakes.

"I was a senior in high school then, a year behind her."

Talking made it easier to sketch without focusing too closely on the result. I told Ed about sending off my own applications and about my dreams of being an art student in New York, dark and broody and brilliant. I told him about my fear of not being able to leave home and about my guilt over wanting to get away. I talked and sketched, and scarcely noticed the tears that had slipped free.

"But Jessica was healthy through the whole year. And happy. And she pushed me to go. She'd been the focus for too long, for all of us, and she wanted me to go. She said I needed to go out on my own and follow my dreams.

"I guess I let her down."

As Ed's chest took shape, there was something wrong. Something was too neat and clean, despite his wrinkled shirt and lightly drooped shoulders. I crosshatched the fabric some more, biting my lip while playing with the shading. And then I lifted my pencil, letting it hover over the paper for a long hesitation before starting on the splotch. It began just below the bottom edge of the page and spread upward, as it had when he'd been lying on his back. It grew in ugly rivulets, staining his shirt and eventually drying in a stiff sheet.

It marred the shirt but completed the picture.

When the sketch was done, I sat for several minutes, staring at the Ed I had recreated. I liked him better this way, living on the page instead of rotting underground. I didn't have to dig up his obituary photo to know I'd gotten him right. This was the Ed who had been a mystery to me, despite our closeness in his final moments. This was the Ed I couldn't forget. But the distant gaze bothered me. It made me wonder what he had looked like before losing his wife. What he might have looked like again, in time. It made me wonder if there would have ever been easy laughter again. If I'd only stayed away.

Day Five

Drawing Ed got easier after that. Alive but stained by a deep hole, slowly oozing blood. I moved from portraits to full scenes. I sketched him sitting on his porch steps, standing in a pool of light at the end of a dark hallway, and walking away from the school. I never drew him lying on the floor. My favorite—next to the first portrait—showed him sitting on a kitchen chair, a bottle of scotch on the counter beside him and a can of soup spilled at his feet.

After a week, I couldn't go on without proper supplies. My last empty pages were filled, front and back. The backs of older sketches, too. I needed a new sketch pad and the tools that could capture the nuances of Ed's expressions. The emotions.

There was a shoebox of supplies leftover from art school somewhere, but it wasn't in my closet, and it wasn't in the boxes I rooted through in the garage. And the more I looked, the more I realized that I didn't want that box anyway. I wanted something new. I wanted supplies I hadn't held before or set down before.

In college, my favorite place in the city had been a small art shop run by a sculptor and his graduate-student daughter who, fortunately for him, was more interested in running the business than in working on her own half-finished oils and watercolors. It was a twenty-minute train ride from school, but I didn't mind. I would sit on the slick plastic seats, when I could, feel the rhythmic trundle, and let my eyes go out of focus. Lost in a hazy image of what I had seen throughout the day. Imagining what I would draw next.

At first, I'd tried to plan my trips for off-times, when I could be somewhat alone with my thoughts. But too few people in a subway car can lead to intrusion. To unwanted advances. It was sometimes better to be packed in, to be lost in the crowd. And some of my best work had come after I'd learned to find solitude in those crowded rush hour rides. After standing with one arm wrapped across my stomach and the other lightly gripping a pole, held upright by the crush of strangers who were just as eager to push through the doors and get back to their individual lives.

At the shop, Remy often worked in the back while Beatrice poured over her ledgers or textbooks at the smudgy, glass-fronted counter. An easel in the corner behind her held a large, unfinished seascape that had been evolving slowly over the course of the year. A new seagull here, stripes added to an umbrella over there. Once a whole family had appeared over a weekend, spread on their tiny beach towels with a picnic basket and a green-and-white beach ball. There wasn't another addition for over a month. And then I was gone, and I never knew if it was finished at all.

Whenever I came in, Remy would emerge from the back room, his hands damp from a hasty rinse and his clothes smeared with clay or spattered with paint. His easy smile and eager hello chased away my fear of interruption—and the chill from Beatrice's corner. He'd want to know what I'd been up to and what I'd seen since I'd last been in. He'd want to know if I'd gone to the exhibit he'd recommended or if I'd found the iron railing he'd described on a certain building uptown. Our conversations were like that. Scouring the world for bits of beauty and sharing them like trading cards.

There was no art shop within an easy drive of my house. Only the big-box craft store with its little bit of everything and its ever-growing selection of scrapbook supplies and silk flower creations. I went there a lot for supplies to use in my classroom. I knew exactly where the drawing and art aisles were, but I never went into them. They made me sad. All those rows of brushes and stacks of canvases sitting idly by while shoppers jostled through the other aisles to stock up on rubber stamps and kid crafts.

My drive there was short by suburban standards. Rows of cookie-cutter homes lined the streets, stretching several roads deep with dotted accents of cul-de-sacs, tot lots, and miniature trees. There's nothing to see but everything to watch as drivers speed, and slow, and cut each other off. Even an easy drive requires more awareness than the rhythmic crush of a subway ride. And there's no subway in the suburbs. No passive transportation that leaves space for a wandering mind.

The parking lot at the shopping center was a massive expanse of lined blacktop, filled with a mix of sedans and SUVs. As I drove in, a pair of women were walking into the craft store. One was in her forties or fifties. The other was much older, probably her mother. Waiting for them to cross, I listened to the blink of my turn signal and watched young families stream out of the pizza place and into the ice cream shop. Most of the kids wore a white martial arts outfit with flip-flops and colored belts of rank.

Inside the store, I hesitated for only a moment before stepping into one of the art aisles with a plastic shopping basket hanging from one arm. Half of one aisle held a selection of pencils, pens, charcoal, and other drawing supplies. The other half was a mix of sketch pads, drawing kits, and instruction books, along with some miscellaneous clearance items. Paints, brushes, and canvases were an aisle to the left, rounding out the store's entire painting and drawing supply. Two small aisles. Sandwiched between the yarn and scrapbooking sections.

The drawing selection felt sterile. Plastic-wrapped products were neatly filed above their labeled prices. Small flags of paper stuck out all around, announcing the weekly sale items. Beside the charcoals, my eyes caught on some boxes of pastels. Pale hues, earth tones, and vibrant palettes. The thought of color slowly seeped in, brightening the sketches in my head. If Ed emerged in color, would his flesh be ashy or sanguine? What medium would capture the viscous red of the blood without blurring the fine lines around his features?

"This one is nice. The blue, see?"

The voice from the next aisle, the yarn aisle, cut loudly through my thoughts, and the responding "Eh" somehow told me it was the mother-daughter pair I'd seen walking into the store.

"Okay, well, he likes red. What about this red one?" Impatience had crept into the daughter's voice. My eyes skimmed across the charcoals and pastels before me, trying to tune them out.

"That one? But it's $5.50!" The mother was as loud as the daughter. Maybe louder. "You know how much that will cost once you buy enough?" She muttered the price again, then started in on how there probably wasn't enough anyway, unless they were all the same dye lot. Which they probably weren't.

"Fine," the daughter broke in with an exaggerated sigh. "We'll keep looking."

I tried to do the same. Tried to keep looking. But even the small selection of pencils and charcoals were starting to swim before my eyes. At Remy's, I never did this alone. He'd show up at my side, pointing out the best. And I'd try them out. There in the store. Remy kept samples around and if there wasn't a sample on hand, he'd pull open a box while Beatrice scowled behind him.

"It's okay," he'd tell her. "We have to make sure it's right, yes?"

Then he'd pull out thick paper and guide my technique as I made careful strokes, trying to feel out the differences from one pencil to another. We'd made a mess of his charcoal demonstration. Ashy smudges all around, and Beatrice shaking her head as Remy insisted I take the boxes he'd opened for a fraction of their cost.

I'd shied away from color in those days, certain it didn't have the impact of a black-and-white portrait, and I hadn't stayed in the program long enough to have that idea challenged. Not by my teachers or by Remy. He would only smile when I complained about school assignments in color. An amused, knowing smile while I insisted that the teachers didn't understand my *vision*. He'd thought he had more time, I suppose. He said I'd be back, and he laughed gently when I wasn't so sure. He'd held his fingers beneath my chin, looked me in the eye and said, "You have the heart of an artist. You take care of your family, you grieve, and you come back. Where you belong."

But I hadn't gone back.

"Just pick something, please." The daughter's exasperation carried clearly between our adjacent aisles. "Here, this one! There's plenty, and it's on sale!"

They bickered about price some more while I ran my eyes along the boxes of chalk pastels, itching to try them out. I'd learned so little about them and forgotten so much. They scared me now. Little blocks of color ready to crumble and blur under my untrained fingers. And then a box of water-color pencils caught my eye. Reassuringly simple. Pencils, but with the option of softness at the touch of a damp paintbrush. A hybrid of painting and drawing. Perhaps.

"Fine," the mother agreed at last. "We'll get this one."

"Thank god!"

I dropped the largest box of watercolor pencils into my basket, taking their overheard conversation as a sign. I was smiling, feeling the same relief that I had heard in the daughter's voice.

And then the mother spoke again, without a trace of humor or regret, but in the most matter-of-fact, conversational tone. "Now, let's see if I live long enough to finish the damn thing."

§

When I got home, George's car was parked in the garage. It was out of place. Or out of time. Parked there more than an hour before it was supposed to be. I sat in my own car for a while, letting the engine run, and sat for a few minutes more after twisting the key. It felt odd to know that he was inside the house, when I should have it to myself before dinner.

It had been strained for a while, after that Jessica slip—though we'd tried to pretend it wasn't—and then we'd fallen back into the day-to-day. Because that's the thing about real life: the mundane chores make it hard to dwell on relationship angst or personal despair for very long. Those dark thoughts seep into the cracks. They eat away and create a wall of sadness. But they can't be front and center all the time. Not when we still need to eat, and sleep, and keep our jobs.

He was in the kitchen when I walked in. I heard him moving around with music playing in the background. His music, not mine. It was easy enough to make a quick detour into the den, stash my shopping bag in the shadowy space behind the leather recliner, and slip back out into the foyer. I made a point of being louder then, while dropping my purse and keys on the table by the front door. As if I'd just walked in. He called hello and I eyed the kitchen doorway before heading in to meet him.

"What are you doing home?"

He was chopping onions but looked up at me with bright eyes.

"Training day." His smile was stolen from a kid on a snow day. "I got out early."

"Oh."

He slid the onion bits into a gathered place, next to a pile of chopped peppers and a small mound of minced garlic. There was a stock pot on the cooktop beside him, sizzling with the sound of ground beef browning. He was making his homemade chili. He liked to cook, when he had time. I liked to order in, when I didn't.

"Where have you been?"

It was a casual question, but I caught a slight—something—in his voice. A catch of curiosity. Like maybe a realization that he didn't know what I did with my time. When he wasn't here. When we weren't being a couple.

"Errands."

It was the easy answer as I reached for a bottle of wine. Red to go with the chili. I brought two glasses to the counter, without asking, and opened the bottle. George watched, and I was very aware of his eyes following my movements.

"Kinda early for that?"

I shrugged and poured one glass, but barely a moment passed before he told me to go ahead and pour him one, too. The way he usually did. I'd taken a deep sip from my glass before seeing his held out for a toast.

"Oh, cheers."

A hasty tap.

There was a movie once, one I don't quite remember, with a scene that claimed the clinking of wine glasses was a way to involve all the senses. It brought hearing into the mix. Smell of the bouquet, taste of the wine, feel of the glass, and all that. It was a kind of flirty moment. In the movie. Said with a lingering look and a promise of something naked to come. This moment didn't feel flirty, or even all that comfortable.

George started telling me about his training then. About the soft-spoken teacher and the rowdy employees who were hard on him. I half-listened while sipping my wine, picturing the blank paper in the den, my new watercolor pencils, and the best way to try them out. Color an existing sketch? One of my least favorites? Start from the beginning and draw something new? How would the colors blend? Should I have bought something else?

"Hey!"

The interruption was loud, with purpose, and I had no idea what he'd been saying. Something about his class. Or something about his boss.

"Should I have stayed at work?" He was half-joking, but his voice was tight. He was speaking with control. The way he often did with me now.

"Why would you say that?"

"Well, you don't seem very happy to see me."

I refilled my glass, even though it was half-full, and tried to think of a fair response.

"You're pacing around like a caged animal," he pointed out a moment later.

Not wanting to fight, I perched on one of the island stools and flashed him a smile. He shook his head at me, as if I'd done something funny.

"It's okay if there's something you wanted to do. I know you like to grade papers before dinner." *I did?* "I'll be fine in here on my own."

But I couldn't go into the den and draw. Not with him so close. Not when he could walk in at any moment and ask what I was doing. Then I suddenly wondered where I'd left my sketchpad, after giving in to exhaustion and going to bed last night. Was it on the chair? Was it closed? I hadn't looked when I was in there a moment ago, but if it had been on the chair, I would have seen it. Probably.

"Are you okay?"

"Uh..." I glanced at the clock, put down my wine glass and tried to smile again. I wanted to appear relaxed, at ease, but I'd forgotten how. "No, I'll keep you company. I just need to check on something."

Back in the den, my old sketchpad was tucked away on the lower shelf. I pulled it out, glanced at the closed door, opened the cover and flipped through my drawings. Anxiety rising. I eyed them cautiously, scanning each inch, from top to bottom and from left to right, as if I'd be able to tell if someone else had looked at them. As if George's eyes would have left a visible trace.

Sometimes it's like that. Sometimes there's a sense of not being alone in an empty room, or of not being *able* to be alone because someone else had been there too recently. It's a memory, in a way, of something you weren't there to see. Or maybe it's just an awareness. An awareness of other people that's strong enough to make you feel like you'll never really be able to be alone. Not when there's always someone there, waiting to intrude. Or maybe it's a crazy trick of an overactive imagination.

It hurts my head to think about it too much.

"Are you alone in here?" A mental question as I looked down at Ed's face, willing the sketch to tell me if George had been in here. If he'd thumbed through the drawings.

And there was no answer, of course.

"Was it like this for you?"

Ed's eyes looked up at me as I imagined his life with his wife. Their arguments, their crossed signals. I imagined the times when maybe they each wished they could be single again. Not forever, but just for a little while. Just so they could have some space to do what they wanted without worrying about how it might affect someone else.

"It's not his fault," I thought the words, silently sending them to the ghost in my sketchpad. "He's happy to see me. To be home early. And I should be glad he's here."

Glancing toward the kitchen, I imagined George chopping and browning and stirring his chili. It felt awful to leave him alone. But it also felt awful to go back to the kitchen when my new art supplies were calling from inside the cage of their plastic bag.

"Show him the sketches," Ed suggested, using an unconcerned tone that suggested honesty had come easily in his marriage.

"It's not that simple." The thought was certain but without reason.

"It's okay to want things for yourself," Ed assured silently, within the safety of my mind. "You can have things for yourself, even if you tell George about them."

I studied him warily, picturing us at a coffee shop, where we'd share a cup after work, like longtime friends. Like maybe he was an older brother.

What would he say if we'd been friends? Did he have friends? Had they tried to comfort him after his loss?

"Joyce loved to knit sweaters." The story would come from him haltingly, as he sipped his mocha and watched me pick at a blueberry scone. "She would sit for hours, needles working away. Sometimes she'd knit in the den, with the door closed and music playing. Because she wanted some time for herself. And that was okay. I understood."

It was hard for Ed to share that way. I knew it was hard for him to talk about that happier time in his life, just as clearly as I knew this entire conversation was only happening in my imagination. I had no idea if his wife knit sweaters and I couldn't actually remember her name. If I had ever known it. But it *felt* like the kind of marriage they had probably had, for him to have mourned her so deeply. An honest and open marriage.

Opening up to George wasn't nearly as appealing. I wanted my drawing and I wanted my secrets. I wanted to have this thing, this one thing, that was entirely my own. At least for a while. At least until I knew how I felt about whatever I was beginning to feel. I put Ed's advice—*his imagined advice*—out of my mind and headed back into the kitchen.

By the time I got there, George had stopped smiling. The music was still playing, but something had changed. I could feel it the moment I walked into the room. Another sensation that comes with the territory of other people.

"Did you reach him?" George smirked. "Warn him that your husband came home early?"

"What?"

He was stirring the pot. The smell of sautéed garlic was light on the air, mixed with chili powder and cayenne. George laughed then. The kind of brittle laugh that didn't have much humor.

"I'm kidding," he said, though his teeth were clenched. "Come on. I come home early and you're acting skittish? Like you're meeting your secret boyfriend or something?"

Was I supposed to laugh? It didn't seem funny. And then George was looking at me with drawn eyebrows and tight lips.

"Unless I shouldn't be joking?"

There was real tension in the air then, building by the moment, but my mind hadn't caught up to this twist of events and everything was beginning to feel hazy and distant, like a dream.

"Are you serious?" It was an honest question, because I could no longer tell.

"Should I be?"

Something boiled and popped in the stockpot between us. George turned the burner down, bringing it to a simmer, and angrily washed his hands. After another sip of wine, I could feel the heat rising in my chest. My stomach was churning. My hands were shaking. He was doing a rain dance with this line of questions, trying to bring on the storm, and I wouldn't give him the satisfaction. I had better things to do. I could be drawing, testing out colors, bringing Ed back to life under my fingertips.

"You're being ridiculous," I think I said, or something to that effect. He wiped his hands on a towel, long after they were dry, and I told him, as calmly as I could, that there was no secret boyfriend, or anything like that. He slowly nodded as I spoke.

"Then what?" His question came after a long silence. "You don't talk to me anymore. You're preoccupied all the time, and then today—it's obvious you want to be elsewhere."

"Which means I'm having an affair?"

The sky split open. I'd tried, but it wasn't enough. The anger washed in then, different than the icy storm but just as overpowering, building and burning and taking away my last shred of patience.

"I'm not allowed to have my own routine? My own plans? I'm not allowed to be thrown when you show up two hours early? You instantly decide that I'm a whore?"

"That's not exactly—"

But I couldn't let him finish. I couldn't hear it. He was wrong. I was right. My drawing time had been taken away, and I wanted my anger instead. I wanted my moment to storm out. I spun on one heel and stomped back to the foyer, snatched up my purse and keys, and turned toward the garage. I could hear him behind me, following, but I didn't want a discussion.

"Just give me some fucking space!"

Once outside, I didn't know where to go. The garage was loud with silence and cold with its bare cement walls. Part of me wanted George to follow and keep me from leaving. The rest of me got in the car, started the engine, and hesitated for just an instant before opening the garage door. I needed a place to think. Or maybe a place to talk.

Day Six

Sitting at Holly's kitchen island felt surprisingly natural. Holly was frosting a cake, piping pastel rosettes and swirled edging. Kelly sat in the adjacent living room, coloring and tearing strips of paper at her small table, and there were drawings and craft projects taped to the wall beside her. The rooms were warm with cheery yellow paint and touches of red. Red like cherries, not like blood.

My place at the island was across from Holly, where an expanse of pale granite ran between us, littered with pastry tips and frosting bags. I'd offered to help, but there was nothing for me to do. I couldn't begin to make the sugary petals which were blooming on the cake beneath her deft hands.

I hadn't expected to go there. Not entirely. But sometimes anger gives you the courage to do the things you really want, even when you didn't realize you wanted them.

With Kelly occupied, Holly had seemed happy to let me in. Happy to have a grown-up drop by her world. She'd put on a kettle for tea and brushed off my weak apologies.

Just showing up, after a hasty text, was apparently okay and I wondered why I'd never known that before.

"How bad was it?" She didn't look up from her work, which made it easier to talk.

"I don't know," I admitted honestly, telling her our fight hadn't really made much sense.

"It rarely does."

Sitting there, I was glad Joe wasn't home from work yet. That it was just us. I gave her the highlights of the fight. The part about George showing up early, the truth about my being irritable and distracted, and the ridiculousness of his idea that I would ever cheat on him. And then I stopped, remembering her confession in my car too late.

"Excuse me." Kelly's tugged on my pant leg, holding out a piece of raggedly cut paper and a doll shoe stuffed with broken crayons. They were mostly greens and browns. "Will you draw me a turtle, please?"

"A turtle?"

"Yes." A solemn nod. "You draw the turtle and I draw the rabbit. Then they're going to have a race."

"Story time yesterday," Holly explained with a smile.

"Ah, sure. Of course!" My smile was wide as I took the shoe of crayons from her tiny hands. I was probably too eager but it felt good to be given a task that would keep my hands busy. A task I could actually complete. "Do you want a real turtle or a cartoon one?"

"A cartoon one?" Kelly's face scrunched up, looking toward her mom as if second-guessing the decision to let me into their home.

"You know, a turtle standing up and running like a person," I tried to explain. "Maybe in a jogging suit?"

Peals of laughter.

"Turtles don't stand up like people! They crawl on the ground. Like this!"

She dropped to the ground, crawling with her back arched and her little head tucked toward her shoulders. For a moment, I wanted to join her. To shrink back to toddlerhood and start my life all over again.

"Okay, I've got it now."

"You can draw that?" She accepted my reassurance and skipped away, then stopped halfway to her table to sternly call back, "Don't put clothes on him!"

I dumped the crayons on the countertop, sorting my own pile of supplies across from Holly's pastry tips. There were three shades of green, two browns, and one blue crayon. They were waxy and chipped with peeling wrappers and the familiar scent of childhood dreams. Holly didn't have to tell me that the blue was for the eyes. Every drawing taped to the wall had blue eyes like Kelly and Holly. Even the police car and the apple tree.

"You could tell me, you know."

Holly didn't have to elaborate. I wondered if part of her wished it were true, so she wouldn't be alone. Part of me wished it was true. It would be something to bond over. Something she could understand.

"I know." My voice faltered, the way it does when I'm too aware of the ways I don't fit in. "And I appreciate that—I really do—but that's not it."

She'd finished the cake and was carefully slipping it into a cardboard box. Soft and light, fragile whorls of sugar in pastel hues. The man who had ordered it would be stopping by soon. He was picking it up on his way home from work, to surprise his wife.

I switched between brown crayons to add highlights to the turtle's shell, not sure when Kelly would be ready for the animal race. I'd expected her to draw her rabbit faster than I could draw my turtle, but she was still hunched over her table, drawing with painstaking care.

"What is it then?" Holly pried gently, and she had the right since I'd shown up on her doorstep. "You said, *'that's not it'* as if there *is* something."

Kelly hummed in the background. The dishwasher churned and sloshed, and Holly watched me. Patiently. She'd told me her secret and was waiting to hear one from me. I'd known it would come to this before driving over. Maybe not consciously, but on some level.

"I'm drawing," I said at last, releasing a shaky breath and setting down the crayon.

"And?" Her confusion confused me for a moment. "You can't talk at the same time?"

"Not this turtle." I held up the finished picture, then dropped it back on the counter. "I mean, that's it. That's the secret thing. I started drawing again. Like back when I was in art school."

"Oh. Well, that's great!" She had every reason to think that, but she stumbled over the words, probably wondering why that would merit secrecy.

"Or it's not great?" She tried again, but Kelly chose that moment to bound back into the room. She held out her hand for the turtle, nodded her approval and asked for two pieces of tape so she could add the drawings to her wall collage. The conversation waited as we watched her dance away.

"It's new," I ventured, "and it's old. And I'm not ready to share it with George. Or with anyone. But it feels really important. Like it's more than what I *want* to do. It… It's like something I *need* to do. That I can't *not* do. And it feels big, maybe even too big… I don't know."

It was a crazy ramble that said more than I expected but not nearly enough. Holly's eyes softened and she leaned in, waiting for more.

"I can't sleep without drawing first," I admitted quietly. "It's the first thing I want to do in the morning, and I think about it all day while I'm doing other things. There's never enough time, but I feel bad taking more time. For… this. For drawing… For…"

For myself. I thought but didn't say.

There was silence as Holly thought about what I'd said, and I loved her in that silence. I loved her for not rushing in and for taking me seriously. Her brows drew together as she pulled a lasagna out of the freezer, loosened the tinfoil wrap, and popped it into the oven. Motherhood had taught her that, along with carrying snacks and sticking to a nap-time routine. She had that knack for going through the motions and checking off her list while her mind pondered the bigger questions.

When she turned back, there was a gleam in her eye.

"Did you know Annemarie's sister runs the Art House, over in Cedar Lake?"

The Art House. Art House. Art House. The name thumped behind my ears and echoed its way into my ribcage.

"Since when does Annemarie have a sister?"

Holly laughed in agreement. "I know, right? They hardly talk, I think. And Karin is nothing like Annemarie. Seriously, like switched at birth. You'll love her."

"I will?" My body shook, understanding her suggestion before it settled in my mind.

"You will," Holly answered in a tone that left no room for arguing. "The Art House is your answer. It's basically half studios and half store. There are classes and workshops, and Karin mainly sells local artists' and her own students' work in the gallery. You've never been?"

Cedar Lake was a small community tucked into an older part of town. Dated buildings, but not historic. Mainly '60s and '70s from the brutalistic look of them. It was not in the best shape, but it felt more real than the identical strip malls on every other street. It had big trees and a few outdoor art pieces. There wasn't much there, but the smattering of shops curved around the narrow edge of a meandering reservoir.

I had loved Cedar Lake at first sight. Loved it down to my bones. But I'd never actually gone into the Art House, and I had only returned to Cedar Lake a handful of times, few and far between. I'd put the entire place out of my mind because loving it had somehow felt like pain.

"I can't just… show up there and take classes."

Holly cocked her head to one side and screwed her mouth into a crooked line. She didn't understand. She didn't see the problem. But then I hadn't told her everything. I hadn't told her how Ed was such a good listener, much better than even George could ever be.

"You can, actually," she answered with great patience. "You can meet Karin and the other artists, then you can spend time with people who share that need to create."

I wanted to believe she was right, but there was so much I'd left unsaid.

"We go to Cedar Lake for date night a lot," Holly went on casually. "Usually to that little Italian place on the water. It's very good. And the first Friday of each month there's live music in the courtyard. That's when the Art House usually has its little wine and cheese things, too. It's where we got that landscape over the fireplace."

I turned to look, and a heavy disappointment sank in. It was a happy landscape in glistening oils. A meadow dotted with flowers. There were fluffy clouds and small figures running hand-in-hand. It could have been a paint-by-number. Something I could look past a dozen times.

But it wasn't bad really.

Better when I got up to take a closer look.

Even better when the details came into focus.

Actually, pretty good.

But, somehow, it was still a disappointment.

Holly didn't notice my reaction. She was feeling the side of the teapot, adding water, and setting it back on the stove for a second round. As she gathered pastry tips and wiped frosting, I realized it was getting late. There wasn't much time before Joe would be home, before the birthday husband showed up for his cake, or before George would be sick with worry. If he wasn't already.

"I'm not sure my stuff would fit in there."

I was being diplomatic, careful not to offend and trying to wind down the conversation.

"There's a ton of art there," Holly promised. "It's all different. Landscapes, abstract pieces, you name it. What are your drawings like?"

There was a moment of hesitation as the words were hard to find. I knew what the drawings meant to me but not what they would say to her.

"They're portraits." The answer was simple, but I hoped my reluctance was showing that they were more than that. "Of one person."

I let my eyes drift to where Kelly was dancing around the living room. She was singing a silly song to the rabbit and turtle drawings, twirling around and around. It had been our background music for several minutes, but it wasn't the kind of song and dance that asked for an audience. It was the kind that happened for itself.

She stopped then, while I was watching, and scampered upstairs, yelling that she had to get her twirly skirt. I rushed to speak while she was out of the room, almost afraid she might be contaminated by what I had to say.

"They're of Ed Dombrowski." It was an explanation of sorts. "Mindy's dad."

Holly stopped what she was doing. A sponge was in her hand and water splashed over empty frosting bowls. She looked at me blankly, but there was something in her surprise that made everything okay. When she spoke, her words were reverent.

"I'd like to see them."

§

When I went home that night, George was reading a book in the living room. The lights were dimmed in the kitchen and the smell of chili hung on the air. He set the book down when I walked in but kept his seat in the center of the couch. The space was tense between us for a heartbeat. And then his eyes melted with the same regret I'd felt on the drive home.

"Have you eaten?" He didn't ask where I had been.

"No." I set down my purse and keys. "Have you?"

"No." He stood then, edging my way. "The chili is still warm, if you...?"

"Yes, okay," I nodded. We were less than two feet apart, our eyes clinging and reflecting *something*. And we stood in the silence. Together. He nodded and headed into the kitchen, trusting that I would follow.

Two deep blue bowls were stacked on the counter beside the cooktop. George began ladling chili into the first one and I glanced around the kitchen, looking for some way to help. The bottle of wine was corked now. The glasses had been rinsed and set beside the sink. There was half of a loaf of French bread in a bag on the counter, leftover from the bruschetta we'd made over the weekend. When I crossed to pick it up, I passed within inches of George's warm shoulder. He handed me a bread knife and I cut thick slices while he carried the bowls to the table.

I arranged the slices of bread on a green plate. He reached down two new glasses and quietly reopened the bottle of wine.

Once we were settled at the table, he again lifted his glass and this time I toasted wordlessly before drinking. The silence stretched around us, making the earlier scene retreat into the past. The words didn't need to be said, but we said them anyway.

"I'm sorry."

"No, I'm sorry."

He began eating and I knew he was holding back. Resisting the urge to rehash and question, the same way he had resisted hugging me when I got home. Because he knew I needed space. He knew I would only feel smothered if it wasn't the right time. But I knew that he wanted the closeness, the connection, and, in that moment, I wanted it, too.

I pushed back my chair and knelt at his feet, wrapping my arms around his waist and letting him pull me into his hard chest. Feeling his sigh as he let his breath escape in a long shaky exhale and enjoying the way he tightened his arms around me while resting his cheek against my hair.

It was warm in his arms, and I felt a release in my chest. Or closer to the pit of my stomach. It was more than letting go of this fight. It was forgiving the earlier hurts. The mention of Jessica we were still avoiding, the talk of babies, and the shape of our future.

His breath moved over me, through me, settling the winds in my head and chasing away the words I had rehearsed on the way home. We stayed that way until my kneecaps shifted for relief from the tile floor. Then George lifted me to my feet, guided me onto his lap and stroked my back. Minutes passed. The silence receded, and the sounds of the kitchen came back into focus. The hum of the fridge. The sudden clink of ice falling into the dispenser.

"George?"

"Mm, hmm."

"I'm hungry."

He laughed, and I went back to my seat, smiling in return. The mood had shifted to what it could have been—should have been—when I'd first come home to him cooking dinner. For once we hadn't dissected an argument or reignited it through over-analysis. It felt good this way and I wanted it to last. I wanted us to eat our chili and drink our wine and not talk about what he'd said, and what I'd said, and what it had meant, and why we'd said it.

As I watched him eating, over my glass of wine, the warmth of his embrace was still strong in my body. His scent was clinging to me. The clean smell of bar soap and laundry detergent, and the deeper scent of his skin. Musky and slightly spicy. It brought back half-formed memories of earlier times. Times of being closer, if not happier. Times when feelings were new and exciting, loud and insistent, but also deep and inevitable.

"Am I allowed to ask?" He said after several bites. "Where you went?"

The warm, happy feeling faltered, and I set down my glass. It was gone by the time I picked up my spoon. It was replaced by the cool contentment we'd grown into over the last few years.

"I was at Holly's," I answered cautiously and felt an indistinct pang when he nodded, showing a slight twinge of relief.

"How's she doing?"

"She's doing well." I poked at the chili, liking its deep brownish-red against the blue of the ceramic bowl. "Kelly's really cute."

And I regretted it before the words were entirely out. A cute child. Holly's baby. We could have a cute kid like that, if we wanted. But George didn't pick up on that line of thought. Instead, he smiled and went back to the story he'd been telling me earlier. About his training class and his boss, or the teacher, or whatever the story had been. And I listened, or tried to, but inside I was also trying to remember the feelings that had come up just minutes before. The warm glow I'd felt when looking into George's eyes. The growing urge to show him my drawings.

But it had passed.

Day Seven

"You're too pale," I worried over the drawing, smudged wine glass in one hand, thin paintbrush in the other. There was no response as I continued to gently dab at the paper. Waiting. Hoping.

I'd shown Holly some of my sketches, and her response had eased some of my fear. She'd said they were beautiful. Soft and gentle but deeply gripping. And her body had relaxed after closing the book, telling me she'd been tense before seeing them. Maybe expecting something else. Something darker. Some awful, disturbing thing that she was relieved to not see in my drawings of Ed.

"When you said you were drawing portraits of one person," she paused to set the sketchpad aside, or to choose her words, "I thought you were drawing Jessica."

The idea should have occurred to me. After that fight with George. After his slip. That was the connection that my brain should have made that night. But it hadn't. Looking at the closed sketchpad with Holly by my side, and Kelly putting together wooden puzzles at my kitchen table, I felt a sense of guilt. Why hadn't I drawn my sister? Why hadn't I brought her to life on the page the same way I'd rescued Ed from his grave? I hadn't drawn her at all since she'd been gone. Had I been too afraid to face her?

The idea wouldn't leave me alone after that. I dreamed about Jessica that night. She was a perfect snapshot memory in my head. Pale, but flushed with laughter. Bald, but smiling through her pain. She had been beautiful in that weakened state, maybe more beautiful than before, despite the ugliness of the disease that was stealing her life away. Not because of the way she rose above, though she did. She was stronger than all of us in those last days. Or she wanted to be—and she seemed to be. But it was something else. Maybe it was the way her essence had been distilled and tucked into tiny places. In the sparkle that lit up her eyes. In the twitch of a smile that appeared in the most unlikely moments. She was magnified in those glimmers. Brilliant and blinding.

I had no choice but to try sketching her as well. Late at night, with a glass of red wine instead of my usual bourbon. Red wine because it seemed like her kind of drink, if she'd stayed in remission and reached twenty-one. Sophisticated but simple. Liked by almost everyone and welcome nearly anywhere. We would have casually opened a bottle over a hand of cards or while watching an old movie. We would have laughed out our days and reassured each other through our fears. We would have been closer then, closer than we'd actually been when she was alive. Back when my adolescent angst and years of high school rebellion had kept us further apart than the cancer itself.

But Jessica didn't speak to me from the soft paper. Not the way Ed had. She looked as if she might. Alert and full of life. The page showed every line and freckle and slightly crooked tooth. There was the small scar from falling off a pogo-stick. There was the tiny remnant of a chicken pox mark above her left eyebrow. But it took time to recreate those details. It was a struggle. There were so many Jessicas in my head, moving with fluid memories. It was hard to pick an expression for a single picture. To settle on a moment to capture.

The first result had been an unrealistic mix of smiling eyes and smirking mouth. Expressive, sassy, but not the Jessica I knew. The second, a thousand-yard stare with a wide, fixed smile. Not even close. It was the third attempt that felt right to me. Crinkled eyes and upturned lips that were eager for outside news. Jessica on a good day. When she seemed on the verge of walking herself out of the hospital. Like she was ready to quit being sick and come back to being the big sister I needed her to be.

It was her on that page but seeing her wasn't enough. I wanted to hear her voice filling my head. I wanted to hear her laugh, or tease, or even argue. I wanted her to rail at me for marrying her boyfriend. Anything really. But it never happened.

Instead, Ed's voice continued to whisper from the shadows. I murmured stories to him as I sketched. Stories about Jessica. About growing up together. I told him about searching our parents' room for Christmas presents while Jessica stood guard. I told him about riding our bikes to the toy store across town, without permission, and getting lost. I even told him about the day in the hospital when she'd introduced me to George and how he'd stayed by her side right until the end. But I didn't tell him how George and I had grieved together. Or how we'd navigated the shame of growing closer through our pain.

I needed some boundaries.

"When do I get to meet him?" It wasn't a new question.

"Why do you want to?"

"He's your husband." The answer carried weight, given his own role in the marriage he'd lost. And when I didn't respond, Ed continued, "If I met him, you could draw in the day instead of sitting up all night."

The thought had occurred to me before, and I'd already found the place where I could make drawing a real part of my daily life instead of a late-night obsession.

Holly had been right.

I'd gone to the Art House on a Saturday afternoon and found Cedar Lake exactly the way I remembered it. Stark buildings, minimal design, yet charming in its way. Even more so on a warm weekend with people strolling the sidewalks and sitting on the lakeside benches. Couples hand-in-hand. Parents with small children.

The Art House was a cement rectangle at the far end of the horseshoe, flush with the widening lake. I hadn't noticed its massive, mullioned windows on my previous visit. Black lines that broke the glass into uniform rectangles on all three floors. The door was red. Painted and stripped to an antique finish. Or maybe naturally worn over time.

Inside, artwork hung on narrow walls that were arranged in an open maze throughout the space. Bins of wrapped prints scattered along the outer walls, amid shelves of ceramics and glassware. Off to one side, near the cash register, a glass case displayed the gleam of handmade jewelry. Signs near the door listed information about the art classes that were held upstairs.

I had no intention of talking to Karin that day. I wasn't going to introduce myself or tell her about my drawings. I wasn't sure what I had in mind exactly, but I'd wanted to see the place. Maybe test what it might be like to step back into that world. And what I'd found made it harder to walk away. Because it was more than a gallery or an art school. Karin had created a community.

The whole shop had that easy, artsy, communal vibe. Karin—who looked enough like Annemarie to be easily recognized—had a relaxed way of talking to customers. She called goodbyes to a trio of artists coming down the stairs, then casually asked a fourth to man the cash register for a few minutes. The other two employees, who wore jeans and paint-splattered Art House tee shirts, helped customers as if they were old friends.

"That one's not for sale." A voice from behind startled my focus from the painting I was studying. "The artist, Benjamin Stolarz, painted it during his last months in a nursing home. It's the only painting he ever made. His only work of art."

The piece was an intricate mural, centered on a short wall toward the middle of the main room. A wash of blues and greens with tiny figures in sweeping processions. Parades of crudely drawn people, highlighted by small clusters suddenly drawn in greater detail. Little vignettes placed amid a teeming mob.

"His wife let Karin hang it, but it's not for sale. I'm Gareth," he held out his hand and a half-smile stretched across his young, stubbled face.

He wasn't wearing an Art House tee shirt, but Gareth clearly belonged to this place. It was in his slouched but confident posture and his comfortable smile. There were paint flecks on his fingernails, on the underside of his wrist, and on an old satchel slung over one shoulder.

"Too bad," I told him, with a nod toward the painting. But then reconsidered. "Or maybe not."

"No?"

I had turned back to the painting but could see his head tilt from the corner of my eye.

"It's the kind of painting that shouldn't be owned."

There was something about that painting. Something intangible hidden in the lines of the figures and in the movement of the procession. Something that captured the journey of life itself, revealing truth without giving any answers or instructions. It held my attention and made the rest of the gallery, the rest of my life, even the storm, fade away. It was calm and quiet. It was deep and cool. Yet focusing on each individual vignette had caught my breath and made my heart race with unspoken excitement.

When I looked up again, Gareth was gone. Karin was finishing up a sale at the register and eyeing me in a way that made me wonder how long I'd been standing there entranced.

"It's a beautiful piece," she said when I walked over to the counter. I agreed and found myself saying that I knew her sister, then telling her about book club, and about Holly, and about Holly's suggestion that I come here, because of my drawings. And it was all out in the open in a moment. Too late to take back.

Karin asked about my school in New York and nodded without questions when I explained that I'd left due to a family matter. There was a lull in customers while we talked, and Karin brought me upstairs to see the studios.

In the main room, large windows and high ceilings offered plenty of light for the scattered easels and work surfaces. Gareth painted behind one of the easels, while two girls worked over a collage on a large table. I flushed at the sight of Gareth, remembering the way I'd spaced out on him downstairs, but none of them looked up when we walked through the room. The second floor held a ceramics studio and a metal shop, each with a few people working on their own projects. I didn't see any teachers and Karin explained that there were no classes or workshops in session at the moment.

"We only have a handful of classes each week. The rest of the time, it's an open studio. Members get their own access cards, but they have to use the back entrance when the store is closed." She walked into the hall and opened a door that led to a small roof terrace and an outdoor spiral staircase. There was a slot for a key card next to the door.

"The ceramics and metal shops aren't open after ten, but the other rooms are accessible 24/7."

The third floor had a lounge area with battered chairs and couches, a fridge, and a repurposed counter with a built-in sink and a well-used coffee maker. Locked cubbies extended beyond the lounge area and a padlocked door led into a closed storage area. While we looked around, one of the girls who had been making the collage, the one with purple-streaked blonde hair and a small spiral tattoo on one side of her neck, passed through with a quick hello before grabbing her purse from a locker.

"Heading out?"

"Yeah, gotta work at two, but I'll be back tonight."

Becca and Jen, Karin told me, were working on an idea for the upcoming art show in Greenville. I assumed one of them—Becca?—was the purple-and-blonde girl and the other one—Jen?—was still downstairs working on the collage.

I didn't ask about the Greenville art show, knowing it would be easy enough to look it up on my own time, without exposing how completely uninvolved I'd become with the local art scene.

When the tour was done, I left with an information packet and membership application, along with a vague idea that I may—or may not—actually find the nerve to apply. The memory of the art available in Karin's gallery/store came home with me as well. Some pieces were good, some were not so good. A few were truly stunning. When my own work merged into that mental mix, my assessment of it was hard to pin down. Was it better? Was it worse? Could it hang on those walls and would anyone actually pay money for it?

At home, I went straight to the den and flipped through my sketch pads with a critical eye. That was two days before Holly came by to see them, back when I was relying on my judgment alone, and I wasn't sure I liked what I saw.

The drawings that had seemed so full of emotion before my trip to the Art House had become flat and amateurish. Cramped and contained on the bound pages. Limited by undeveloped technique. They seemed feeble attempts. Better than average, perhaps, but not great. Not art.

"What makes a portrait art?" Ed had asked, as I flipped between penciled watercolors and my earlier sketches.

"The realism." The answer was quick to come, but I thought about it further, trying to quantify. "The light and shade. The details. The little touches that get overlooked in daily life."

I'd stopped thumbing pages while I thought about the question. When I glanced down, the pad was open to my second sketch of Jessica. The one with the distant eyes and forced smile. The one that I'd initially thought I'd gotten wrong. As I looked at it again, *really* looked at it, I saw something else. A new side of Jessica. It was a side of my sister I hadn't wanted to see when she was alive, but one I may have always known was there, underneath her brave face and overcompensating smile. It was the side of her that was isolated with her pain and all too aware of how truly alone she would be—we all would be—in the end.

Engrossed in the picture, it took a moment to realize that Ed was still talking, trying to be heard above my other thoughts.

"Art isn't any of those things," he said when I finally listened. "It isn't the light and shade or any special technique. Art is the emotional connection. It's *your* emotional connection."

But I could only shake my head and insist that he was wrong. He had to be. Because I knew that I'd always kept my guard up. That I'd never truly, deeply connected to anyone in my life.

Something happened when I started drawing Ed. Something that shifted the storm in my mind. Drawing Ed somehow made the storm quieter, less confining. But there was something else, too. Bringing Ed back to life, on paper, made him more than bleeding flesh and breathless body. It let me experience him alive and well. In a way. It let me imagine his life before. Times when he was happy with his wife and daughter. Times when he was sad, grieving, and angry—but still breathing.

Reaching into the past with Ed, even through my own imagination, brought his daughter into the present as well. For three-and-a-half years, Mindy had been eight years old. She'd been hopscotch and ponytails and shyly sounding her way through reading circle. I'd thought about drawing her—with Ed or on her own—but I couldn't, because she wasn't that little girl anymore. She was now eleven. Or twelve? She was growing up. She was living out in the world. Each day, she was growing and changing and becoming a different person than the one I'd briefly known.

When I replay that day now, I'm often outside of myself. Not just watching myself go through those awful moments, but sometimes hovering even farther out. Sometimes I'm settled in Mindy's bed and behind Mindy's eyes. Imagining the feel of the pajamas on her skin, the weight of her sheets and blankets. There's a doorbell. There's yelling and a sharp crack. There's my guidance counselor, storming into the room with wild eyes and reaching arms.

What was Mindy thinking in that moment? Was she weak with fever? Had she thought it was a dream?

The bowl of hot soup on her bedside table said that Ed had been taking care of her. Maybe she'd been happy to have the soup and to have three days at home with her dad. Maybe she'd been sad to be sick without her mom there to put a cool cloth on her forehead and sing her to sleep.

When I recreate that day from her perspective, the walls always fade away. No matter how hard I try, I can still see into the living room where Ed—*where my dad*—lays bleeding while my teacher hovers over him, helplessly begging him not to die.

Maybe I can't stay within the walls of her room (a place I've never been) because her confusion and fear in that moment is too horrifying to comprehend. What had she been feeling during those moments of not knowing? Was there anything in those frenzied moments? Could her mind even speculate beyond the shock?

I can picture her just after, cowering in Liz's frantic embrace, and then with the police, being gently led (or carried?) to a waiting car. I can picture her aunt and uncle sweeping her into tearful hugs. But those are only made-up pictures. They're from a story that may or may not match the reality of that day. And even if I'd been in that room, right by her side, I still wouldn't know how those moments had been processed in her small body.

Eight-year-old Mindy was trapped in my memory. Just as grown-up Mindy felt poised in my future, ready to someday look me up and come asking for answers. But drawing Ed began to change that certainty. Why would she come to me with questions? Wouldn't her family help fill in the gaps? Or would she she fill in the blanks herself? Would she write her own story, shaping and refining it with each passing year?

If she wanted to meet anyone someday, it might be Liz. Mindy might want to see for herself, ask for herself, know for herself. That idea scared me. To see Liz would mean going to a sad place and seeing the misery of damaged minds on full display. It would mean wondering if that's where she might be headed herself someday. Because Mindy was broken, too—by the events of that day—and that's what broken people feel when facing an outward show of damage. They wonder and compare. They imagine what straw could break to send them over that edge. And they wonder, if they were to fall, if they would ever make their way back.

With young Mindy held in my memory, and grown Mindy haunting my future, I had to force my thoughts to the Mindy of today. To the real, breathing, growing Mindy. I looked for her one night, online, and found a handful of social media profiles that were locked down fairly well. There was nothing to see but her name and a single profile picture. Either her substitute parents—her aunt and uncle—had taught her to be safe, or she'd gleaned that lesson herself. Learning to be guarded. Especially around those who claimed they were there to help.

Her picture was enough though. For me. It showed the same soft brown hair and lightly freckled cheeks. She was older and prettier. Her lips were closed tightly, maybe hiding braces, but stretched in a smile. Even if the smile didn't quite reach her eyes. There was an arm around her shoulder, and the long hair of friends on either side, showing that her face had been cropped from a group picture. That made me wonder most of all. It was good if she had friends now. Unless those friends gave her aunt and uncle a false sense of security. Did they see Mindy with friends and stop worrying? Did they think she had adjusted? That she had healed? Did either of them know what it was like to put on a smile and act the way you were supposed to act, even while feeling the cracks spreading inside?

I didn't tell Ed about finding her picture. I couldn't. He was in the past and she was heading into the future. Mindy would grow older, but Ed would never see it. He would never dance with Mindy at her wedding or hold her future babies. To Ed, Mindy would always be eight years old. Just as Jessica would always be 19 to me. And to George.

§

A week had passed since my visit to the Art House. Another week of late-night drawing and bleary mornings. It had become a new routine. Work, draw, dinner with George. Wait for George to go to bed, then draw until my eyes burned and my wrists ached. Draw until the hour was late enough to scare me into getting a few hours of sleep.

That routine couldn't last. The school year was coming to a close and the open summer was looming. For the first time, I hadn't made plans for teacher development training or alternate work, and my drawing beckoned. The Art House beckoned.

A new plan had begun to take shape. A plan to spend my days at the Art House until my next year of third graders. And maybe then it would be easier to develop a healthier routine. A new schedule that would bring my drawing into the light. That was the tentative plan I'd tested out on Karin. The idea of spending my summer in rediscovering my love of art made sense. It felt safe, even if I was gearing up to make a big, scary change toward something better.

And then I lost my job.

Getting fired came as a surprise, which it probably does for most people. It makes sense to feel surprised when your life is being changed without your input. To feel blindsided and wonder if you missed a sign that it was coming.

When Jason said he was *letting me go*, I don't know what I felt. If I felt anything. I do know that I thought about a blue toaster. I didn't mean to, or try to, it was just there. An image of a blue toaster distracting me from Jason's next words.

It was a specific blue toaster that came to mind. One that had shown up during Jason's first year as principal, back when he was still finding his way and we were still sizing him up. He'd come into the teacher's lounge one day, when a few of us were sitting around during recess, glad not to be on playground duty. As soon as Jason entered, Philip had started pushing for new music books and Bonnie began asking about upgrades for the classroom computers. I'd kept on eating an English muffin, straight from the package and dripping with honey.

"How can you eat that cold?" Jason had asked, after eyeing me for a few minutes.

I'd shrugged. The lounge had a small refrigerator, a microwave, and a coffee maker.

"No toaster."

It wasn't a complaint, just a statement of fact.

The conversation went back to school budget demands, and I finished eating with honey dribbling down the side of my hand. The next day, there was a new toaster—bright blue—sitting on the counter next to the coffee maker. Jason never explained it, but I knew he'd bought it for us—for me—with his own money. Maybe it was a small gesture to make up for the larger balancing act that left each of us short on classroom supplies. Maybe it was something he'd chosen to give because it hadn't been a request.

Or maybe he'd just been amused by my answer.

I had to shake away the memory before I could process the news that he was letting me go. Firing me. But it was persistent in hanging on. That blue toaster.

"Do you want to know why?" Jason sounded tired then, worn out by a conversation we hadn't yet had. And I said,

"Okay," though I wasn't sure I really wanted to know. Or that a reason would really matter. It just seemed like the thing to say.

Jason sighed, raised and dropped his hands, then looked around the room. He shook his head and lightly bit his lip. This was hard for him.

"Well, that's a pretty good start."

I didn't know what he meant, but his next question made it clear.

"Do you even care about losing your job?"

It seemed like an odd question to be asking. Was I supposed to reassure him that I was hurt? Did he want to know that I felt at least as bad as he did? Fortunately, he didn't need my answer to continue.

"Look, I've really tried, since the... incident. I fought to bring you back because you were a good teacher and because you'd been punished enough for one bad call. But the last few years, you've just... I don't know."

He hesitated, maybe giving me a chance to jump in, to correct or reassure, but I didn't want to interrupt his train of thought. It was a different side of Jason than I usually saw. Less reserved. Less polished and together. I was suddenly very interested in what he wanted to say. Maybe it was a chance to see what I looked like from the outside. To someone else. To someone who had been officially tasked with observing me.

Though it also felt odd to think that he'd wrestled with thoughts of me. That he'd spent time thinking of me at all. Even if it was his job.

"You're here, but you're not," he said at last. "Your students still like you, but you aren't engaging them the way you used to. You're distant with the staff and you do the bare minimum outside of the classroom. And lately...

"I don't know. I thought things were getting better, even if you were distant, but over the last two months... I just don't know."

He didn't say, *"You don't eat English muffins in the teacher's lounge and crack jokes during recess anymore."* But he might as well have.

I'd taken to staying in my empty classroom instead. At first, it was to avoid the judgment and questions, and later it continued out of habit. It was easier that way. To keep some distance. Maybe not using his toaster anymore had been the final straw.

"And I'm not the only one to notice." He was in the middle of a sentence, making me realize I'd missed something while thinking about toasters and their possible double meanings.

"To notice?"

Jason's eyes were sad as he slid a folded pamphlet across the desk. Simple black print on pale yellow paper. Folded in thirds. It was information about alcohol and drugs. About the warning signs of addiction.

I couldn't pick it up. My face felt hot and my eyes stung as it lay on the desk between us, but everything else, every other feeling, was oddly quiet. It wasn't the pamphlet exactly. Or it wasn't the pamphlet alone. It was something else he'd said that was beginning to catch up with me. Something about things being different in the last two months. And that triggered something I couldn't quite place. It was a silent accusation that screamed in my ears. The kind that brought dark clouds and the threat of rain.

"You're an adult," Jason said gently. So gently that it was hard to make out the words. "You make your own decisions and what you do when you aren't at work is your own business. But it's starting to bleed in, and even if it weren't, as a friend…"

He went on then. Rambling that I looked exhausted, that I was sleepwalking through the days. That I looked like hell. And what do you say to that?

I could have told him that maybe there had been a time, not so long ago, when I'd sat up drinking until the storm in my head died down enough for me to sleep. And I could have told him that I was barely drinking at all anymore, just one glass to nurse through the night, and some nights none at all. I could've explained that it was the drawing that was keeping me up all night. That it was saving me. That it wasn't an escape like the bourbon had been. And that I had a plan to move forward. To make it better.

But I didn't say any of that. Because what if it wasn't true? What if the drawing was just another escape? Another substitute for being a healthy, feeling, responsible adult? And what if my plan fell apart? What if I couldn't pull it off? What if it was a narcissistic indulgence? What if I had no talent at all?

I sat there, not saying any of it. Listening to his words but thinking my own thoughts. Waiting for the swirling dark whisper to rise around me with the howl of a storm. But it didn't. It became calm instead. Not like the eye of the storm, but more of a sweeping void. An open field of quiet, like I'd felt while studying Benjamin Stolarz' mural at the Art House. Feeling everything and nothing at the same time. A muted chaos in the calm.

When Jason said my name, again, I knew I should respond. But there was nothing left to say.

It's strange knowing you'll never go back to a certain place. A place that had been a significant, solid part of your day-to-day. It's hard to imagine that place still existing and moving on without you, instead of being frozen in time. It was like that with the school. It was strange to accept that I wouldn't go back, and it would go on. To know that someone else would teach in my classroom and the teachers I knew would keep teaching in theirs, without me there. Eventually, they'd grow older and quit, making room for new teachers to come in. New teachers who would never know me and never know that I was the reason they had a blue toaster.

I sketched that toaster when I got home. Tucked back and alone on a Formica countertop. I colored it a vibrant blue and shaded the background in quiet grays. Later, I gathered up the sketchpads and stacked them on the kitchen island, leaving them to wait while I preheated the oven and started making dinner.

I talked to Ed while I sketched. I told him about the meeting with Jason and the sense of failure I'd felt. I told him about the blue toaster and the pale-yellow pamphlet. It felt different to talk to him while sketching something that wasn't him. In some ways, it was easier. Not seeing his eyes or the set of his lips made it more like talking on the phone. Like calling a friend who would keep any secret.

"Were you ever fired?"

"Of course," he answered quickly, reassuring that everyone had been fired at some point. Even if that wasn't true. I wondered what he'd done for a living before he'd died. His career hadn't come up at our only real meeting, and if it was mentioned in the media aftermath, it hadn't stuck in my mind.

I could have looked him up online, plugged his name into a search engine and sifted through whatever came up. There might have been some old hits that weren't tied to his death. There might have still been an online obituary, maybe even one of those funeral home pages with comments from friends and family. The kind of thing that I could pore over and let each message tear into my heart. But that's not what I wanted. It was enough, and maybe better, to imagine his life—his career—based on his appearance. On the look of his house and the way he had dressed. It was enough to let the words flow and see what came out.

"It was my first job, after college."

His story began haltingly, as the toaster took shape. I corrected the perspective of the extended countertop, listening patiently. "Architecture is a competitive field, and my boss wasn't above stealing the designs of his youngest employees."

The story was trite, but the idea of him as an architect was a soothing fit. A creative job, probably well-paying by that time, would account for his well-appointed living room and single-malt scotch.

"And you stood up to him?"

I imagined the scene: young Ed, talented and idealistic, protecting his designs from an unscrupulous hack. But picturing it brought in memories of sitcoms and TV dramas. Similar storylines that were clearly fictional and raised too many doubts.

I gave up on a backstory, bringing the conversation back to the present.

"Something like that," was enough of a response to dismiss the details of his story and move on without losing the sense of conversation. I was getting good at that sort of thing. His words went on, skating around the details. "My point is that it happens sometimes. To the best of us. And it doesn't have to be a bad thing. Sometimes it's a push in a new direction. A better direction."

I agreed with a quiet nod. It was what I'd told myself on my drive home. I could spend the summer looking for a new teaching job and abandon my plan for the Art House. Or I could double down on my plan, diving into my art and taking this turn as a sign that it was time for something else. Something better.

But I had doubts and reassurance from an imaginary Ed wasn't making the plan any easier to accept. I did know what might help though, if I were to be honest about it, and that thought came to me in Ed's voice.

"You'll feel better after you talk to George."

He was probably right—*I* was probably right—but until George got home, even the idea of telling him made my stomach clench with dread. Even if I *wanted* to talk to George about it, I didn't know where to begin. Start with my previous plan for joining the Art House over the summer, then work in how I'd lost my job? Or start with being fired, then show I already had a new plan? Was there a right way to explain it?

I'd thrown around some ideas with Ed while sketching and kept the practice conversations going while making dinner. There had to be a way to make George understand that my heart wasn't in teaching anymore. If it ever had been. I was even a little relieved that it was over. Though I did wish I'd stolen that blue toaster on my way out.

§

George came home just as I was pulling the salmon out of the oven. Rice and vegetables were in serving bowls on the island and the table was set. I'd lit the votive candles that sat in a cluster at the center of our small table and poured two glasses of wine, despite the memory of the pale-yellow pamphlet I'd left on Jason's desk. The sketchpads, which had distracted me the whole time I was cooking, had been moved out of the way but were still ready to be shared. When the time was right.

"Mmm, smells good," George said as a greeting, smiling at the domestic scene. It was something that only happened on the good days, when my head was clear.

"Well… yeah… um…"

The hopeful happiness on his face made me want to tell him fast, before he could anticipate something good.

"I'm not a teacher anymore."

I slid the salmon onto a platter with a weak smile.

"What?" His smile faltered but didn't fade entirely.

"Nice," Ed mocked sarcastically in my head.

"I was let go today. Fired." I tried for a reassuring tone, ignoring Ed. "Should we make up plates?"

George stared at me. Something in his gaze tried to connect, but he was caught off guard. He didn't understand. Which was understandable.

"That's how you tell him?" Ed's annoyance was growing, while I stood like a mannequin with a painted-on grin. *"Seriously? This isn't a breezy thing. Get over there and tell him the right way."*

With a sigh, I left the serving fork next to the salmon and walked around the island to a place where I could step close and hold both of George's hands.

"Tell him how you feel," Ed prompted needlessly.

"I know." I nodded, brushing away the distraction of Ed's words so I could focus on George. Our eyes met, and my stomach churned. "I didn't see it coming either."

George squeezed my hands then, encouragingly, even as his eyebrows bunched together in concern. Some flicker of emotion passed over his face, as if he were also deciding how he should feel.

"That sucks," he said at last.

"Yeah, it kinda does."

We stood there together, not saying anything, just thinking it through. Ed was quiet, too. Giving us space.

"Are you okay?"

I was prepared to be calm and in control, the way I'd practiced with Ed. I was going to tell George about the Art House and assure him that I was ready to move on with a better future. Instead, the tears welled and his arms pulled me close, rocking us both in a slight side-to-side motion. He murmured words of concern and reassurance until I was ready to pull away and pull myself together.

With a shaky breath, I handed him a plate and began to fill my own. I needed a task in a moment like that. Something to take up the open space while I reined in my emotions and breathed through the gathering wind. Salmon, broccoli, rice. A neat display against the blue of the thick ceramic plate.

"It's okay," Ed reassured. *"You're doing great. Keep telling him how you feel."*

He was right, and I tried to find a smooth segue from the tears that had surprised me to the exciting plan that I desperately wanted to share.

"It's still kind of… I don't know… strange."

George made up his own plate, added an extra dash of pepper and met me at the table. We began to eat, and I told him what Jason had said. Mostly. Paraphrasing. Summing it up by saying that Jason didn't think I was the right fit anymore. That he thought I'd been different since coming back. That I hadn't been as involved as he liked. But I didn't mention the pale-yellow pamphlet.

"Maybe this is a good thing," George said after a pause, unknowingly echoing Ed's reaction—*my* reaction. "Maybe it's time for a change."

"That's what I was thinking."

My eyes drifted over to the waiting sketchpads, and I weighed the feeling between us, sensing whether it was the right time even as Ed whispered in the background, spurring me on.

And then George threw the conversation off its tracks.

"It could be a good time to try therapy."

"Therapy?"

I don't know why I was surprised. It wasn't the first time therapy had come up, though it was the first time in a long time. We'd been through it all before. The reasons to go, my reasons not to go. His not understanding and the ensuing arguments. Broaching it now wasn't one of the conversations I'd practiced.

"I know you haven't been sleeping lately."

That was true. I had an answer now, but he continued before I could tell him why.

"For a while, I thought it would get better. Or that it was slowly getting better, over time. But in the last few weeks… It's more like it was in the beginning again. You're not sleeping. You're more distracted."

He didn't know that the progress he'd thought I'd made before had all been a sham. That I'd been pretending through the days and keeping the thoughts and memories from everyone—even from myself—as much as possible. He didn't know that all of that was different now.

"Tell him," Ed whispered in my ear. *"Tell him, now."*

But how do you explain something like that? Something that should be simple but feels much bigger than any words can express? My plan was something more than the explanations rattling through my brain. My plan was simple in words but complicated in emotions.

"Just talk!" Ed began demanding, yelling in my head. *"Stop making it such a big deal and just say it. Just say 'I've been up at night drawing' and 'I want to get back into my art' or something like that. Anything like that!"*

But Ed's badgering was too loud. It drowned out the words I could have said and made the winds churn through my head. I could see the stack of sketchpads across the room. George had walked past them without noticing. They were right there. Waiting. I could pick one up and hand it to him. Let the drawings start the conversation. See what George would think. But then I'd see what George would think.

And there was something else, too.

Jason and George had both noticed that something had changed in the last few weeks or months. And it had. I'd started drawing. I'd started connecting to Ed. But why? Why then? The question echoed, making something in me quake. What had changed? Why had it changed? Did it matter? Did I know then what I know now?

I still don't have an answer.

"Just think about it," George spoke softly as he put his hand over mine. He was trying. He was being there for me. I couldn't dismiss that, even if his trying had gotten in my way. Even if something about it had made my chest ache, and my head throb, and had made it harder to say what I'd wanted to say. Even if it had somehow left me feeling more broken than ever.

I nodded, managing a weak smile, and left the sketch-pads out of sight.

"Coward."

§

Two days passed before I mustered enough nerve to pull out the Art House packet. I told George that I wanted to take some classes and sign up to use their studio space. I said I wanted to get back in touch with the art I'd left behind. Flipping through the glossy brochure, George nodded in thoughtful agreement.

"You've already filled out the application?"

It was a question, but George was holding up the completed paperwork as he asked.

"Yes…But I wasn't going to submit it before talking to you."

George shook his head and raised a hand, as if to say that wasn't what he meant, then skimmed over the details printed at the top of the page.

The waiting felt like torture. I wanted George to agree immediately. No questions asked.

"I know it's kind of expensive, and I won't be working now…"

"No, it's not that. It's-- I mean, I don't care about the money." But he cared about something. It was all over his face. Questions, concerns. Speculations he didn't voice.

"Show him," Ed whispered. *"Show him everything."*

My mouth started to open, on the verge of offering up my work, but then George smiled and said that I should do it. That he thought it was a good idea.

"I can come by to see the place with you this weekend."

"Oh."

I hadn't expected that. Not his offer, but the reaction that came with it. I hadn't expected the feeling of uneasiness that had been brewing throughout this conversation to suddenly solidify in the pit of my stomach.

"Well..." I gently prodded at the uneasy lump. Was it fear? It was something in that emotional family, but its shape was thick and heavy, without clear form or intent. "I'd like to maybe keep this for myself right now. At first, you know? But after I get settled in..."

"What are you doing?" Ed jumped in, clearly annoyed. *"Bring him. Show him. Go get your sketchpads! Now."* His voice was loud, but the growing lump in my gut, the shaking fear, was more insistent.

"Oh, uh, yeah. Yeah, sure." George was flustered but recovering quickly. "No, I get it. It's fine." He smiled and squeezed my arm, trying so hard to say and do the right things.

"It's not fine," Ed pleaded with me. *"He's hurt. You're shutting him out and he's hurt. Why are you being such a coward? Why can't you just talk to him?"*

Ed's words became muffled as I forced him out, willing all my focus on settling my queasy stomach and slowing my choppy breath.

Breathe in. Breathe out. Smile.

George and I stood together, smiling and nodding. Awkward, but awkward together.

"I'm proud of you." George spoke with a sincerity that made me step in for a hug. His hands smoothed down my back and I closed my eyes, feeling my inner world begin to settle. This was good, I told myself. This was a big step. A right step. Though I still hadn't shown him my sketchpads.

Or told him about Ed.

Day Ten

My dreams about that day are always fragments. Detailed fragments that mix themselves up or work their ways into other dreams. The crack of a gunshot. Fingertips touching an outstretched arm. Warm blood. A glass of scotch. Dark hardwood floors. A child crying.

The dreams are less frequent now. Less persistent now that I have more time to myself. Time without the strain of worrying how I appear to others. How I affect others. Now that I've made space for looking inward and wading through how I express my memories, both inside my head and outside to others.

But when the dreams do creep in, they come with those same scattered fragments. A jumble that makes erratic leaps through time. A muddle where disconnected scenes bleed into other, unrelated moments of memory, or fantasy, or speculation. Whatever you call that subconscious retelling that happens during moments of restless sleep.

It's only when I'm awake that the day replays itself in the right order. When it does, it replays slowly, frame-by-frame, reconstructing, recreating each detail. The memory unwinds carefully, giving my mind time to fill in the hazy blanks of moments that happened too fast. Whether those blanks are filled with fact or fiction is anyone's guess. Though I like to think the recreation is true. Or mostly true. Or true enough. And there's no one left to contradict it, so maybe truth doesn't matter all that much.

The memory of that day can start replaying from any point, but when I try to start from the beginning, it unwinds from the moment I parked my car in Ed's driveway.

We'd driven up to the house around 4:15, not long after school let out. The sun was shining between banks of gray striped clouds, casting a pale glow over the white columns and warm bricks. The door was edged in black, its faceted glass shot through with metal accents. There was a bucket of sidewalk chalk on the edge of the porch and a tangle-haired doll sitting on the front steps. She was wearing a tiny white sweater and had no shoes on her feet.

Liz had walked ahead grimly, without so much as a glance at the doll or the chalk, and pressed the doorbell with a solid jab. She was wearing a green sweater that was pilling around the waist and a pair of gray slacks with a falling hem on the right leg. Her black purse hung by her side from a cross-body strap and its zipper gaped open, perhaps in a way that would have exposed her small handgun, if I'd bothered to glance inside. I'd left my own bag in the backseat of my car and carried a folder instead. Mindy's schoolwork. Things she could have worked on when she felt well enough. If the day had gone differently.

The doorbell sounded inside the house. My stomach flipped as a shadow approached the frosted glass, knowing we shouldn't be there. Or maybe I only remember it that way now. I was nervous about being there and unsure if it was overstepping. I remember gripping the folder of papers more tightly and hoping Liz would let me talk first. I'd wanted to frame it as a friendly visit to bring Mindy's schoolwork and keep her from falling behind, but Liz's quivering jaw had me worried that she would say something else. I was afraid that our visit would be seen—correctly—as a flimsy excuse to check up on them.

That's what I'd been afraid of as I stood on Ed's porch. I was afraid that checking up on Mindy might be too intrusive. I was afraid that Ed would be offended. I hadn't imagined anything worse. Now I can't imagine being that naïve.

Liz had been quiet on the drive over, not replying at all when I suggested that I lead the conversation. She had nothing to add when I said we should be friendly, polite, and very subtle in looking for warning signs that might help the case worker. I wanted her steely silence to equal agreement, so that's what I chose to believe.

When the door opened, Ed greeted us with a resigned sigh. He wore a blue button-down shirt, untucked over black jeans and dark socks. The glass of scotch was in his left hand and his right rested lightly on the edge of the door. His socks stick in my memory. They made me feel embarrassed for showing up at his home without warning. Without respect for his privacy.

"Hi, there!" I launched in with my bright and cheery teacher voice, prepared to keep up the shameless ruse that it was normal for us to be there. "We just wanted to bring by Mindy's school work so she—"

I didn't get far before Liz lifted both arms and pushed hard against Ed's chest. He was a big man, but the unexpected shove made him stumble back just enough for her to stomp into the house uninvited.

"Hey!" He hurried ahead then, cutting her off, and set his glass on the coffee table.

Clink!

I followed too, surprised and confused but desperate to catch up so I could diffuse whatever scene Liz was about to cause.

"And you're drunk." Liz pointed toward the scotch as if the single glass proved her point. "Again!" Her face was red with anger. Her eyes were wide and there was something different about her expression, a look I'd never seen before. It was a naked pain that stopped me in my tracks and choked off my hasty apology.

"Excuse me?" Ed glanced from her to me, his mouth parted in disbelief.

"You think you have everyone fooled," she raged at him then, wild-eyed and out of breath. "But *I* know. I know what you're doing, and I'm not hiding it anymore!"

"Doing? I don't—" Ed swung his gaze my way, and I raised my shoulders, silently pleading for him to know that this was a surprise to me as well. It was still in my mind then—the idea to step forward, to apologize to Ed and usher Liz back out of his house—but the intensity of her pain had left me frozen in place.

"You promised you wouldn't hurt her," Liz's voice changed then, suddenly sounding young and vulnerable as tears ran down her cheeks. Her shoulders drooped, her head dropped forward, and her arms hung limp by her sides. Her whole body was trembling. A quiet tremor that seemed to vibrate throughout the room.

"All right, that's enough." Ed turned his tired eyes my way, shaking off his momentary shock. "Take your friend out of here now, or I call the cops."

I can feel myself nodding, about to move, when it all becomes a blur. A tangle.

Liz suddenly held a gun, leveled toward Ed's chest. His eyes widened with an alert terror. An expression that I often see in my dreams but hadn't wanted to capture in any of my drawings.

This is the part I replay over and over.

This blur of events snags the flow of the memory and flashes behind my eyes at odd moments. Every repeat of these few moments feels like it holds just a tiny bit more. Like there's something hidden in the choppy gaps and misplaced details. An important something I can't quite remember. Some small detail—or maybe something larger—that changes, or *would* change, or has the *potential* to change everything.

These moments repeat again and again. Scanning and searching and trying to uncover some hidden truth. Some missing piece. Or pieces.

How did Liz pull the gun out so quickly? How had she gone from angry to defeated to murderous in the span of less than a minute? How did I not know that her purse held a gun? What was I doing—what was Ed doing—in the precious seconds it took for her to become armed and dangerous?

Liz stood just a few feet to the front and side of me. Her arms were outstretched, shaking and gripping the gun with both hands. Ed had his arms raised, palms forward, while his eyes darted between me and Liz. I could see his mind churning through things to say, options that might make a difference, but my own mind was lagging behind. It was a struggle to take in what was happening—that it *actually was* happening—let alone think of an action to influence the event.

My brain still thinks that long, agonizing moment didn't really happen. It tries to tell me that Liz, someone I considered a friend, hadn't held a gun and pointed it at an unarmed, unthreatening man. My brain also thinks there's still a chance to change the outcome. As if we're all still there. Maybe my brain thinks it can tap into an alternate universe where I *am* still in that moment. Where I still have a chance to decide what to do. What to say.

My brain insists on going through the options, testing out scenarios, even while another part of my mind tells me that it was real. That it did happen. That it's too late.

I see us all in that room, in my memory. I see myself, too, but from outside of myself. As if it wasn't me standing there but another person, an innocent, unbelieving witness.

I can't retrieve the memory of how that moment looked from behind my own eyes, though I know that perspective must be inside my head somewhere.

"I haven't hurt Mindy. I haven't hurt anyone."

Ed's voice was gentle, careful, as he tried to reason for his life, but Liz cocked her head to one side and twitched with tiny jerks. Her eyes blinked as if trying to make sense of something. It was as if she were listening to something else. To some other words playing out in her head.

"You said if I went along, if I was good, you would leave her alone. You promised. And I was good. I didn't tell. I went along, and you—"

Her words choked off, disappearing into convulsive sobs.

And now the memory comes back from inside my own body, though I can see us all from the outside as well. It's a sort of superimposed video as my feet inched toward her. My lips whispered her name. The world stopped. There was no one else. It was just the three of us, thrown into that unreal moment.

Ed's next words didn't register at the time, but they became embedded in my mind, and play on a loop through most of my dreams.

"Who do you think I am?"

And then the gun went off.

Crack!

Ed was about to crumple to the ground.

I was about to run toward him.

Liz was on the verge of seeking out Mindy's room.

But there's a snag before those things happen. A snag, or catch, in my memory that pulls me back to those final seconds before the shot fired. Something that makes me consider, and reconsider, all the things I could have said or done. All the things I might have said or done. All the things I did say and do.

There's a snag in my memory. It's a sort of airless, question-filled gap. There are no answers in that pause, but it's still the moment where a part of my brain decides, with utter certainty, that Ed's death was my fault.

Day Eleven

I felt like an outsider on my first day at the Art House. An intruder, a sham, or a kid playing dress-up. I felt like the new kid at school, except without the structure of teachers or a class schedule to organize my movements.

It was about ten when I showed up on that first day. Ten o'clock on a Friday morning. A time when most people were at their nine-to-five jobs. Just a week before, I'd have been teaching math. I thought the studio might be empty at that time, but there were more *others* than I'd expected. People who worked off hours, later shifts or weekends. People who didn't work another job or otherwise had the time on a Friday morning to draw or paint or sculpt or find their own way to create.

Karin pointed me to an empty cubby for my belongings, explained that I could bring my own supplies or buy them from her at a discount, and then headed back downstairs to the store and gallery below. The third-floor break room was quiet, and I was alone to find my own way. No assigned first-day buddy in the adult world.

The click of my padlock was loud in the stillness, and it came with the panicked thought that I might not remember the combination. *12 right, 27 left, 4 right.* I hadn't used a padlock since high school. Just the weight of it in my hand, the look of it, brought back the smell of pencil shavings and cold metal lockers.

Downstairs, in the main studio, there were four people quietly working on their own projects. Two of them wore earbuds and none of them looked up when I entered.

Becca was there again. The girl with the blonde and purple hair. She was snipping photographs at a back table. She'd start by snipping around the subjects, then carve out accent lines and fine details with a pen knife. When she laid them out on solid backgrounds, bright colors seeped through, showing each person in a subtle new light. It was unsettling and energetic, beautiful and slightly unreal. I tried not to hover, not to stare, as I fumbled through my bag at the neighboring table.

The others were working at easels. With oils. With charcoals. With acrylic paints. The easels were arranged in a large U shape, facing inward at an empty space where I assumed a model would be during classes. There were glances my way as I moved toward the empty places at the base of the U and settled in front of the center easel, leaving a buffer on either side, but no one stopped what they were doing to say hello or ask who I was or what I was doing there. No one broke the working silence. I took their cue, trying to make as little noise as possible. Trying not to disturb.

I set up a Bristol board and lined my supplies on the narrow side table.

Then stared in fear.

The blank canvas looked too white in this wide, open space. Too empty. It had been too long since I'd worked at an easel, instead of being curled and cramped in my leather chair. The vertical board seemed more like a wall to climb than a space to fill.

The people working comfortably around me were a silent audience, despite their apparent indifference. I could feel their awareness of me, and it felt like a mistake to be there.

"Do they know you're a murderer?"

Ed's voice shook me. He'd never called me that before. Never blamed me. But before I could piece together a response, he went on. *"That's not me, that's what you think. That you don't belong. That you killed me. That they'll be disgusted when they find out, and they won't want you here."*

He wasn't wrong, but I only partly believed that. I also believed it wasn't my fault. That I'd done my best.

"But which way will they see it?"

I swallowed hard, aware that standing in front of an easel without drawing was making me seem even more out of place. I rummaged through my bag for a sharpener and made a quiet show of prepping some pencils, inspecting and honing points that barely needed sharpening.

"Which way do you see it?" It was the first time I'd asked Ed a direct question like that. The first time I'd probed for his reaction to his own death.

There was no response, of course.

Ed retreated, and I knew I had to start drawing. But instead of making my first mark on that waiting canvas, I switched it out for a smaller sheet of paper, torn as quietly as possible from a sketchpad in my bag. It was more familiar. A better place to begin.

But I couldn't raise my pencil.

I stood still for minutes that felt like hours. My mind as blank as the paper itself. My mouth dry and palms tingling. Sweat warmed my forehead and low back, while a gentle nausea gathered at the back of my mouth.

I willed myself to close my eyes.

The soft shushing of brushes and snipping of scissors filled the air. There was a dull thud when a painter knocked something solid over on his table. My eyes snapped open, but I didn't look his way. I let my eyes go soft again as I listened, breathing slowly. There was an easy warmth and the memory of a place that wasn't quite like this but was near enough. I let my body relax into those sensations. I let the smells of paint and chalk and ink mix around me, as the morning sun streamed in from the large windows.

It was perfect.

When my eyes came back into focus, the rest of the room disappeared. A few sure strokes and Ed's familiar gaze floated in the center of the paper. His voice, kinder now, whispered encouragement in my ear.

"Welcome back," I thought in greeting as his features took shape. My breath slowed. My shoulders relaxed. It was easier to let go—of the strangeness and the strangers—once

my body was in motion and my own whisking strokes were adding to the symphony of the studio.

We didn't return to my earlier question. We didn't talk at all, exchanging our silent thoughts. Instead, I let Ed's face emerge with gentle eyes and perhaps a hint of forgiveness in his smile.

Sometime later, a woman on my left put down her charcoal and crossed the room to stand beside another painter. She moved quietly, but her motion was enough to bring me out of that hazy, timeless flow. Glancing around, blinking to reorient, I saw that a woman toward the front of the room had left and another had taken her place. The back table was still scattered with Becca's photographs, but Becca was nowhere in sight.

They kept their voices low, but the whispered cadence drew my eyes back to the woman and man chatting beside his painting. The woman caught my gaze and smiled warmly.

"Coffee break?"

I followed their lead by leaving my supplies at my space, though I hesitated to leave my drawing—to leave Ed—in the empty room. Unfinished and exposed. It was an act of faith. A risk toward fitting in.

We climbed the stairs and found Becca sprawled in an armchair, sipping tea from a patterned mug and staring into space. Her earbuds were still in place. It reminded me of our common room in college, but with no TV. A communal settling in to share space and swap stories. Like the teachers' lounge, but with no blue toaster.

Charcoal woman had a name—Doris—and the painter introduced himself as Bill. Doris was a few years older than me, a stay-at-home mom whose kids were in middle school. Bill was retired and rediscovering a childhood hobby. She had an emotionally distant husband who might be having an affair, and he had a son who hadn't spoken to him in two years. But those were things I learned in later conversations. On that first day, it was more about learning names and catching the rhythm of the group.

At first sight, Becca seemed both the odd one out and the only one who truly fit in here. She was young, barely into her twenties, and had the expected look of an artist. Tattoos, piercings, and purple hair. A paisley jumper over striped tights. I felt pale beside her in my shorts and baggy t-shirt, bland and drained of personality. A suburban soccer mom, but without the kids. My plainness was a better fit with Doris and Bill, who looked like they should be out shopping with coupons or feeding birds in a park. Yet I didn't know them, and they didn't know me. And it only took a few minutes to see that those outside differences were nothing compared to what was below the surface.

As soon as we arrived, Becca pulled out her earbuds to razz them both about missing some class the day before. Doris rolled her eyes and draped across her chair as if she were twenty years younger, and Bill came back with a laughing comment about Becca needing more help with forced perspective than they did. There was an ease of general adulthood. An agelessness and melting of social barriers. These people knew each other and had bonded.

Being new, I'd expected to be a topic of conversation. Where I came from, what I was drawing, why I wasn't at a job on a weekday. But none of that came up.

Instead, Becca launched into complaints about the skeevy manager who kept putting her on the night shift. Doris segued into news of the uptight PTA mom she'd finally escaped until fall. While they talked and laughed, occasionally shooting explanations my way, I curled into the couch and sipped gently at my hot coffee, relaxing into the role of accepted observer.

It was Bill who drew me into the conversation. Not about my personal life or my art training, but about a water tower on the outskirts of town. The water tower had been in the news since the city had decided to paint it blue—a hideous, dingy blue with sad blobs of yellowed white that were supposed to be floating clouds. He turned to me, when there was a lull, leaned over with his bright eyes trained on my face and—entirely out of context—asked, "How would you paint that water tower?"

"Vermillion."

I'd already considered it, many times, and decided that there was only one color that would look right against the surrounding trees and shabby buildings at the edge of town. "Solid vermillion."

"Vermillion," Bill repeated the word with a nod and flashed a wide smile at the others before adding, "Okay. I like this girl."

"*See,*" Ed encouraged, *"you do belong here.*"

And I hoped that wouldn't change.

§

At dinner that night, when George asked me about my first day, I wasn't sure where to begin. I could tell him about the morning light that filtered through the large windows and the swishing sounds of people at work. I could tell him about that steady click of confidence I'd felt when I'd looked at my first half-finished sketch and set it aside to start over on the larger Bristol board. Instead, I went the easy route and told him about the people.

I told him about the coffee breaks and getting lunch with Doris and Bill at a sandwich place around the bend of the lake. I described Becca's carved photographs and how Karin kept a large stash of red licorice behind the counter in the gallery shop.

I even told him about the water tower and earning Bill's grinning approval.

George laughed, encouraged by my happiness, but his praise brought a shadow of doubt. Did one good day mean anything? Was I starting fresh or running away? Was I reinventing myself or filtering myself into another manufactured me, and would it all change once they knew what I'd done?

I spent another three days at the Art House before I saw Gareth again.

It was awkward when I saw him, remembering how I'd lost myself in that painting so completely during our first meeting. Yet, on the other hand, I couldn't remember that painting—still can't remember it—without feeling the sense of calm that had come over me on that first viewing. That stillness that comes over me each time I see it. And Gareth was a part of that first discovery.

He was younger than I remembered. Home from his third year of college and working in the bowling alley for the summer. (Facts I learned from Doris over a fourth cup of coffee.) He got along with everyone, offering smiles and friendly greetings, but he also held himself back.

At first, I thought his distance was because he was an actual art student, at a proper college, while the rest of us were nudging our way through self-taught techniques. But it wasn't that. He had a quiet reserve that cut him off from everyone. Kept him at a safe distance from the world. It could have been his natural personality, but I suspected it was a learned response. *Equally broken people.*

For a few more days, we nodded hellos at each other and left it at that. Once, when I was taking a break with Doris and Becca and Bill, he came upstairs and stopped short in the doorway. He wandered in, made a pretense of getting something from his cubby, then hurried down the stairs. Other days, he was more open, sharing a laugh over whatever story was being told, before making his hasty retreat.

Finally, there came a day when we found ourselves alone in the main studio.

I'd moved on to a bigger canvas by then, recreating an earlier sketch of Ed on a much larger scale. I was trying to capture the same emotion of the smaller piece but was feeling less than successful.

"It's the boy," Ed suggested in my mind.

I tried to ignore him, but nothing in the drawing was coming out right. His face was lopsided, his hands were too small for his body, even his eyes were uneven.

"*You can't concentrate,*" Ed pointed out, when an overly wet brush smeared his stubble into the shadowy smear of a beard. "*You're thinking about that first day, in the gallery. You're wondering what he thinks of you.*"

I said he was wrong. Why would I care about that?

"*Because you were vulnerable in that moment,*" Ed was quick to reply. "*Because he was there when your guard was down. You were vulnerable in front of him, and now you're worried that he thinks there's something wrong with you. Or maybe you're afraid he looked you up after that, and now he might know.*"

My skin tingled, but I insisted that wasn't true.

"*Fine, you're afraid you were rude, and he now thinks you're an unfriendly bitch.*"

"Gee, thanks." I didn't realize I'd muttered those last words out loud until Gareth looked my way.

"Did you say something?"

That was when I noticed we were alone in the studio. I wasn't sure when the others had slipped out. They'd been so quiet. Or I'd been so lost in my work.

"Oh, sorry, nothing." I heard myself stammer. "Thinking out loud."

I tried to pick up where I'd left off with my damp paintbrush, stepping back to look for an area to soften next, but I was too distracted by the awareness of the time that had passed since I'd started. It was that strong sense of waking up—of being too aware of the room around me—that told me it was time for a break, whether I wanted one or not. I set the brush down and stretched my arms overhead.

"Can I show you something?"

It was a quiet question as Gareth gestured toward his own canvas. He was nervous but eager, and he glanced toward the door as if making sure we were still alone.

I walked over with a carefully held smile, not knowing what to expect. Maybe something abstract, with bold lines and shadowy figures. Or something dark and twisted. Out of balance and overreaching. Maybe something clichéd in its youthful attempt at controversy. Because maybe a part of me wanted his properly trained art to be awful. Because maybe I was jealous.

I wasn't prepared to see a painting of myself. But there I was, inside the canvas, standing in a blurry gallery and staring at an abstract painting. A look of wonder was on my painted face, while a ray of sunshine created a delicate pool of light around painted-me and the canvas that my painted-self studied. As I looked closer, I could see it wasn't me exactly, but the likeness was enough for me to recognize that day in the gallery. There was an intimacy to the moment. A rapture he'd managed to capture, reflecting the relationship between an artist and those who view his art.

"Damn," Ed whispered in my head.

It was good. And it was humbling, on many levels.

"I don't know what to say," I finally admitted, when the silence felt like it had gone on too long.

"That's okay," Gareth laughed, misunderstanding my meaning. "I'm not sure what I think either."

"No, I like it. Really." I was gushing then. Overcompensating. "It's very good. Rather meta."

He studied me, looking for signs of honesty, while I cringed at what I had said.

"But meta in a good way?" He laughed again, unsure, and I promised him that it was meta in a very good way.

"And you don't mind? That I painted you? Without asking?"

"Oh, no." The answer was quick, instinctive, polite. "Not at all."

But there *was* something unsettling about it. Something that was always unsettling about seeing yourself through another person's eyes.

"Actually, I've been feeling bad about that." I waved toward the canvas, trying to change the subject. "About that day we sort of met."

"Really? Why?" He was genuinely surprised, looking at me so intently with his young, innocent eyes that I wished I hadn't mentioned it.

"Well, you were being friendly, and I just kind of zoned out and ignored you."

"Oh. No," he shook his head emphatically, lips pressed together. "I'm the one who should apologize. I shouldn't have interrupted you. It was just… Well, you were so deep in the painting and I wanted to… I don't know."

We were both uneasy then, but somehow drawn together in the discomfort. Our eyes met. I saw the crack that separated him from the rest of the world looming larger than ever. And then he leapt across the divide.

"You remind me of my mother." He blurted the words quickly. Raspy and urgent. Like he had to say it fast—before the moment passed.

"My real mother," he continued. "Not in the way you *look* so much, but in the way you look at art, you know? Like you've fallen into the canvas."

The crack in his voice when he said *real* mother, the reverence in his tone, clenched my stomach. I wanted to interrupt. I wanted to tell him not to equate me to someone so special. I wanted to warn him that he would come to regret that association. But I was too busy bracing for the words he would say next.

"She died when I was twelve."

There was a pause and I nodded, preparing myself for a story I wasn't sure I wanted to hear. I would listen though, if he needed to talk. I would be there for him. The way people are. It was the least I could do. But then Gareth shook his head and smiled, perhaps thinking better of it, and let the distance begin to settle back into place between us.

"My dad remarried though, and my stepmom is great, too, in her own way."

"I'm sure she is."

"Jesus," Ed interjected his annoyance, but in my head where only I could hear. *"Stop making this about you and say something to the kid! Ask about his mom! Say that he must miss her. That it's okay to miss her and still love his stepmom. Just say something, damn it!"*

But I choked. The feelings were there. The empathy. The sympathy. The understanding. But the words wouldn't come out, and I wasn't sure they should come out. Sometimes being there is letting someone have their distance.

"Well, it's a great painting."

I spoke the words slowly, attempting to put every ounce of feeling into my eyes so my gaze might tell him that I did know what it was like. That he wasn't alone in his grief. That I would be there if he did want to say more. And that I would be there if he didn't.

It was the best I had to offer.

§

Why am I retelling this? Why do I keep going over these particular moments? Maybe it does help—this writing down whatever comes to mind. This retelling. Maybe it puts the pieces together. The pieces of how I got here. The clues of where I might be going when my time here is up. Or maybe I'm still just stuck in the past.

Day Twelve

My book club isn't a literary society. It's a book club in the laid-back, stereotypical sense: a semi-regular meeting for drinking wine and catching up, while loosely talking about a book that almost everyone has at least partially read. We don't discuss the technical merits of plot pacing, and purple prose, and whatever things literary types discuss. Instead, we stick to our simple impressions, the why we like or don't like a book. The what it makes us think about. It's an easy chatting that veers away from the book and back again. Dipping into personal stories, both old and new.

Most of our time is spent on non-book conversations. Some are light and others are more serious. There's talk of parenting, marriage, in-laws, and jobs. Also talk of politics, and sports, and local news. Shopping, and restaurants, and charity work. There's talk, and wine, and more talk. It's something I used to like. Before. It's something I wanted to like in the years after. And now…?

We've been meeting for years, some of us since college. It's always been once a month, and lately we've stuck to the first Thursday of every month. It's easier to have a set day of every month. Most of us are able to plan around it, except when we can't. I rarely miss a meeting and I always finish the book. It's a point of pride. Or maybe just a habit. Another routine. I even read the book for last week, knowing that I couldn't possibly be there.

I used to talk more, before, chatting about cute or trying students, about George or my parents. Chatting about all those things that felt good to let go. But that easy chatting dried up after Ed died. My sharing shrank to thoughts about the books but nothing personal. I became more of a listener. An observer. It felt more natural that way, which makes me wonder if my previous chatting had felt natural before. Had I become more myself or less?

After settling in at the Art House, something began to shift. As I got ready for the next book club meeting, an urge began to surface. It was an urge to share. To tell these women—my friends—about the Art House, but also about losing my job. Maybe even tell them about sketching Ed, about discovering this new relationship with him. It was an urge to tell them the things I still hadn't told George. But I didn't know where I would begin, or if they would understand. Or if I would regret saying any of it the second the words came out.

Maybe I always felt that way, and I only think it felt different before. Maybe it's a basic social anxiety, the kind of thing that a lot of people feel, and there was always an awkwardness in speaking up and being on display. But maybe it didn't bother me as much then. Maybe it had been easier to push aside when I was only marginally cracked, but it's harder now that I don't trust my decisions anymore. Not just decisions about the big things, but even about small choices of words and expressions and body language. I second-guess myself and assume my broken mind will make choices that are out of step with the expected actions of a well-adjusted adult.

Those are the fears that keep me from settling in with the easy laughter around me. Social events are minefields. One minute you're relaxing into the conversation, the next you're saying something that brings a look of confusion, or discomfort, or pity. Maybe it's safer to keep distance and remember that I'm different. Maybe that's why, when listening to chatter in social gatherings, my brain likes to slip in dark and unrelated statements like, *"I watched my sister die a slow, painful death."* Or, *"I held a man in my arms and watched his life bleed out around me."*

Those out-of-place thoughts come without reason or invitation. They make me feel different. Removed. Separate. Maybe I'm not the only one who's experienced trauma, but maybe I am the only one who hasn't learned how to fit those experiences neatly into my past and move on, wiser and stronger, the way healthy, well-adjusted people do.

I don't know if that's a stumbling block or an asset in my new world.

On the day of that last book club meeting, I tried talking to Ed about it, while sketching to calm my nerves, but he couldn't seem to grasp the problem. It was too simple to him.

"Tell them, don't tell them. What does it matter? Why do you care what they think?" And if that's what *he* thought, then maybe *I* didn't think it should be such a problem either. Not really.

§

Holly drove me to that meeting. She'd texted last minute and offered a ride, which seemed like the perfect chance to get her opinion, but we didn't talk about the Art House or my scattered career on the way there. Instead, Holly talked about Kelly and the trouble she'd gotten into during her last week of preschool. She'd hit a boy because he hit her friend and had been punished along with the boy. Holly was livid. She'd told off the director, taken Kelly for ice cream, and then gone to the nearest dojo to sign Kelly up for karate lessons.

I like Holly's kind of mothering.

Her story lasted all the way to Beth's house, and I wanted to listen. To be there for her, but more than that, to be part of the story, even if it was after the fact. Going to book club together, hearing about her life, was what we used to do, and it was nice to have that back, even if it might not last.

Once the car was parked, Holly unsnapped her seatbelt and opened her door before noticing that I hadn't moved at all. I wanted to smile and hop out, but my questions were still echoing. I still hadn't decided what I would share—what I wanted to share—once I went inside.

"You okay?"

And I could have told her then, laid out my fears and gotten her advice, choosing Holly over the imaginary ghost in my head. I could have met her halfway.

I even toyed with the idea of asking her to tell everyone for me. Like back in middle school, when there was always a friend to tell a boy you liked him or to break his heart when you didn't. But we weren't in middle school anymore.

Ed's voice whispered, *"I could tell them."*

I shrugged, trying not to visibly roll my eyes at Ed's offer, and told Holly that I was fine.

When we went inside, the conversations were already flowing. We joined the throng of voices that filled the room with stories of lousy workdays or bad commutes. We poured wine and caught up, oohing over the spread of appetizers and aahing over the platter of fancy cookies. No one noticed that I was quiet. No one knew that I was fidgeting for a moment to speak up, or that I had anything new I wanted to share.

Why would they?

The words almost came out when Emily asked if I was enjoying my summer break—the typical teacher question— but before I could form an answer, Beth began reining everyone in to start talking about the book. There was a scramble, a rearranging of seating to form a ragged circle, which shuffled me to the far side of the room from Holly and Emily, leaving me perched on a dining room chair with Beth on one side and Annemarie on the other.

The book that month was a historical novel. One of those fictional retellings of scarcely documented events in real people's lives that are pieced together from letters and journals, then bound up by the author's imagination. The many blanks filled in with assumed conversations, assumed motives, and assumed feelings. It was a story told about real people who'd never had a chance to explain what they'd written in their private journals and letters. People now immortalized in ways that might not capture who they had really been.

It was an uncomfortable book I wouldn't have read on my own, though everyone else enjoyed it. They gushed on, while I half-listened, not all that interested in participating. My thoughts were elsewhere. On my art. On what people would think of me being fired and what assumptions they'd make if I didn't explain the situation myself.

"Well. You have a lot of free time now."

Annemarie's strident tone startled me, the way it often did, even when my mind wasn't wandering. Smaller groups had broken off from the main discussion, and everyone else was occupied in animated conversation. It was just me and her. Annemarie lifted a cookie to her mouth, her eyes smiling (or smirking?) as she waited for an answer.

"End of the school year," she prodded, when I didn't respond, and I realized she was talking about school being out for the summer.

"Uh, yeah." I hesitated, partly because I didn't know how to begin and partly because a glint in her eye made me wonder if she already knew more. "I guess."

"But you're painting now?" Annemarie chewed slowly, and my heart began to thud in my stomach.

"*What the hell?*" Ed snapped. Or was that my own thought? It was hard to tell sometimes. "*Did she talk to Karin about me?*"

"Painting?" The question slipped out of my mouth, followed by a breezy answer that didn't sound like me at all. "Oh, no, I've never been much of a painter. Although I have been experimenting with watercolor pencils lately, which is a little like painting. I guess."

"Art is said to be very relaxing. Therapeutic even." Annemarie arched an eyebrow, reached for her wine, then eyed my nearly empty glass. "Need a refill?"

She had a way of twisting things like that. Comments that would be friendly from someone else came from Annemarie with a layer of judgment and, more often than not, a hint of condescension.

"Art? What about art?" Beth chimed in, reaching for the bottle and casually pouring into my glass before refilling her own. "Didn't you study art once? At some art school? Before switching to education?"

"She's joined up at the Art House now," Annemarie answered for me. "You know my sister's little group of *artists* over in Cedar Lake?"

"Oh, that's wonderful!" Beth beamed. I sat quietly between them, wondering how Annemarie could hold her smile through such heavy sarcasm and how Beth could appear to miss the insult entirely.

"I wish I had time for a hobby like that," Annemarie continued with a frown. "But my job leaves no time for anything else. I barely even have time to read, let alone dabble with paints. Oh, did I mention that I'm up for a promotion?"

And that was the end of my sharing.

§

Back in the car, there was a moody silence as Holly drove me home. I'd been even quieter the rest of the night, thinking about the easy conversations at the Art House and the way Doris, Bill, and Becca had seamlessly drawn me into their small circle. Had it ever been like that at book club? Had it changed after Ed, or had I always been talked over with patronizing smiles?

"What's up?"

Holly broke the silence at the next red light.

"Nothing."

I didn't mean to say *nothing* in that voice that really meant *something*, but even I heard it come out that way.

"What did Annemarie say?" Holly asked with an eye roll that invited me to lay it out for her, and the answer that came to mind wasn't about feeling left out, or talked over, or unable to share my news.

"She said art is therapeutic."

It was a much bigger confession. Holly hesitated, perhaps responding to the weight of my tone more than the actual words.

"Art *can* be therapeutic, sometimes." She spoke slowly, considering.

"True." I offered another confession, "I haven't shown George what I'm drawing."

Holly kept her eyes forward, waiting for the light to turn green.

"Has he *asked* to see them?"

There was a pause then, because it felt a little unfair to answer honestly.

"Well, no." I resisted the urge to make an excuse, to say that he was probably respecting my privacy. Which might have been true. Or not.

"Do you want to show him?"

There was another pause, while we followed a line of cars to the next intersection.

"He sent me an email," I began instead, because I didn't know how to answer directly. "It was an article called, *Art as Therapy*, and it was all about how art is used in clinical settings to help express emotion. And how it could help those recovering from trauma or depression. He wanted me to read it, so we could talk about it over dinner."

"And…?" Her question was neutral, gently probing.

"And… That's what he thinks my art is. That it's just… therapy. Just a way of processing my life."

Holly frowned. She didn't get it, but I didn't mind because she was trying to get it.

"Isn't that what artists do? To some extent? Process life through their art?"

"Well…" She had a point, but George's approach had somehow felt diminishing. The way my parents had often diminished my art.

"It's like he's saying this is temporary," I explained it to Holly slowly, explaining it to myself as well. "Like I'm damaged, and he sees art as a process to fix me, like a cast on a broken leg. Like I'll spend some time drawing, get over my issues, and go back to being a happy little schoolteacher. Start a family and become… normal. Or whatever."

Her head nodded in the dark of the car, her profile lit by passing headlights and her eyes fixed on the road ahead. The nod was slow and thoughtful, more like a sign of processing what I'd said than actually agreeing with me. I swallowed hard and noticed the tightness spread across my chest while I waited for her response.

"So, if he wants you to *become normal*, that means you aren't normal now?" It was the kind of question a therapist might ask, and I remembered that Holly had once majored in psychology. Among other things.

"I guess."

"Broken."

Ed whispered the word in my head, reminding me that I really thought I was broken.

"Besides, he doesn't see art as a real future," I added, looking around at the other cars and mindlessly wondering where they were going, what they were doing out on this random Thursday night. "He never did."

"Do you?"

I shrugged. I wanted to—I *want* to—but it was hard to see a path forward. Maybe it's still hard to see a future, even now that a path of sorts has opened up.

"He doesn't mind me doing it now, since I was fired, and since it's basically like therapy to him… Or like a hobby. Like Annemarie said."

It wasn't an answer to her question, but Holly let it go. She was very quiet for several breaths.

"Do you remember when we met?" She asked at last.

Junior year of college. Spring term, at an open mic night. We were both there as friends-of-a-friend to support some guy that neither of us knew. He was dating Holly's cousin and screwing my roommate, though we didn't figure that out until much later. That night, we'd gravitated together, since we both hardly knew anyone there, except for her cousin and my roommate—respectively—and they were both too fixated on the jerk in question to spend much time with either of us.

"Do you remember what we decided that night?" Holly continued.

It had been years ago, but the night gradually came back to me. The tiny club with the bad acoustics and cheap drinks. The table of music majors who all knew each other, but not us. Holly and I both struggling to understand their inside jokes and shared stories, before eventually moving to the bar to get away from their senseless—yet somehow exceedingly important—talk about Dorian mode and diminished sevenths.

"Sometimes it's fine to be the odd ones out," I drew the memory out slowly.

"Sometimes better than fine," Holly agreed, with an exaggerated look of horror at the memory of that night. "Besides," she added. "You're never really the only odd one out. There are always others who don't really fit in either. Wherever you are."

"And when you're lucky, you notice someone else who's left out and make a new friend."

It made me smile, remembering more of our rather drunk conversation from that night. How we'd leaned in close to yell over the mediocre singing, and the way my roommate had been pissed that I'd spent the night laughing with Holly instead of applauding the jerk she'd dragged me there to meet.

"We never planned on being normal or on fitting in," Holly reminded me. "In fact, I seem to remember a lot of conversations about there not actually being one single *normal* for anyone to be."

"Yeah…" She was right, but that was back when we were young and full of dreams and swearing that we weren't going to end up in the suburbs, living the kinds of lives we were living now.

"So, if there's no such thing as normal, why can't you just do what you want? Make your own way? And maybe tell everyone else to fuck off?"

I was quiet then, looking out at the row of identical houses as we eased our way down my tree-lined street. It was before 10, but the sidewalks were empty. Most of the windows were dark except for the occasional bluish flicker of a TV screen. Holly pulled into my driveway, looking at the house as if she knew what I was thinking.

"Do you know why I decided to have a baby?" She sounded irritated, a little indignant, though she was the one to bring it up. "It wasn't because our parents wanted us to, or because our friends were having kids, or because

I thought it would fix things after that stupid affair. It was because Joe and I decided that we *wanted* to be parents. It was what *I* wanted.

"It's the same reason I quit my job and started baking cakes," she continued with even more fire. "I did it because I *like* baking cakes. Baking cakes makes me happy."

I nodded then, showing that I understood, but that wasn't enough for her. Holly turned to look me straight in the eye and pointed a finger at my chest, jabbing the air for emphasis and pinning the moment in my memory.

"If you don't want to be a teacher, then don't be a teacher. And if you want to be an artist, be an artist. Don't let other people tell you what you *should* be doing, or what you *should* be getting out of it, or how it *should* play out. Just be an artist. Do what makes you happy and see where you can take it."

And so I did what I should have done weeks ago. I went inside and showed George every one of my drawings, letting go of my fears and expectations.

Day Thirteen

Why *am* I retelling all this? That bit about book club. That part about settling in at the Art House. All that stuff about friends and sharing and feeling left out. Is it because I have so much time alone now? Is it because Holly came to visit yesterday? Or because George is on his way to visit now? Is it the therapy stirring up more than I realize?

A lot of this seems like a distraction or a digression. Stuff that's irrelevant to the main story I'm trying to tell. But maybe it isn't. Maybe all of this is part of that same story, and maybe my therapist is right when she says everything that comes up is important. Maybe it isn't a digression at all. My story, like any story, is more than a straight line. It has twists and bends that add shading and depth. Side stories that inform the decisions. That explain, to an extent, even if I'm not sure of their relevance yet.

I do know that there's more to life than the big moments. The traumas. The heartaches. The death. There are all these other complicated things. The social. The awkward. The figuring out where you belong and what you can, and should, and might be doing with this life that you never asked for but are now responsible to live. And those things are important, too.

Maybe those day-to-day things are what actually matter the most. Not everyone has held a dying man in their arms, but everyone deals with the struggle to fit in.

§

Showing George my work was something that had to happen eventually. It felt like the right thing to do. I'm not sure how I thought he would react or how I *wanted* him to react. But his actual reaction was confusing.

Seeing my portraits of Ed, and of Jessica, encouraged George's belief that my drawing was therapeutic. More than that though, he seemed to think it was important in other ways. As if it could change everything that had gone wrong between us. He'd held his breath at the many iterations of Ed. He'd reached out a trembling hand at the sight of Jessica. He'd praised the emotion, the passion, in each drawing and agreed that I should let Karin display some of them at the Greenville Art Show.

Once my drawings existed for him, he wanted them to exist for the world. As if they would mean something and be as important to others as they were to me. And, apparently, to him. Maybe I should have found that encouraging, but I didn't. Instead, it felt threatening. It felt like he didn't understand some fundamental thing that I didn't know how to explain.

It felt like pressure.

George wanted me to tell my parents about my art. He thought I should send them a portrait of Jessica. He said it would be good for my relationship with them, and that made me wonder if he thought repairing that relationship would somehow strengthen our own. Whatever he thought, George saw something in the portraits that gave him hope. He said we'd toppled into a dark rut since the shooting, and it was time to climb back out. I wasn't so sure it had happened that way. There may have been a toppling, of sorts, but I didn't think we'd had that far to fall. I thought it was more likely we'd been edging our way into that rut, bit-by-bit, since the day we'd met.

I knew better than to send a portrait to my parents.

Our family was never the same after Jessica died, if it had ever been truly strong before. The dynamics were off. The heart of the family, the *point* of the family, was missing. The relationship that remained, after Jessica died, was fragile in a way that was better left undisturbed. Once we'd found a tentative calm. A cordial impasse.

My parents had fallen apart—spectacularly—during that first year without Jessica, and they'd gotten back together—shockingly—a few years later. They'd moved away since then, to a sunny beach home in Florida, and now acted as if none of their years apart had ever happened. Not for them, and not for me.

But those years had happened.

The three of us had scattered in those first few years, despite my leaving New York to be closer to home. I understood, in a way. They'd struggled to create lives that didn't revolve around hospitals, and treatment options, and saving Jessica's life. They'd stumbled after failing that common goal. And they didn't see me in those years. Not really. They didn't see how I'd struggled with transferring to a new college. Or how I'd stumbled my way down a safer path, never quite realizing that I was giving up my own life to live out the life Jessica had lost.

My parents' reunion had coincided with my finishing college. They'd called it a graduation present, but it wasn't much of a gift. They'd shown up at graduation with smiles and plans to move south, where they'd start over in sunshine. They'd beamed when George proposed over brunch, and everything fell back into place with a simple click.

We married. They remarried. We bought a house in the suburbs. They bought a house in Florida. The dust settled, and we were all set up in our new, separate lives. There were a few visits at first, then the time between trips stretched from months to years. It stretched without specific animosity. Just stretching the way time does when everyone is busy with jobs, and housework, and grocery shopping, and social media, and everything else that eats away at the minutes and hours and years.

The phone calls continued sporadically. Lengthy but with little substance. They'd tell me about their garden and social clubs, and news of old friends I didn't remember. The same clichés all aging parents and their grown kids hash and rehash. Except when it came to health. They'd never talk about aches and pains or other medical issues. Maybe they'd had enough of doctor-talk, or maybe they didn't think any of their experiences could compete with what they'd watched their first-born daughter endure.

They never explained, and I never asked.

Jessica, however, was not off-limits. They would talk about her as if she were still around but just out of reach. Maybe traveling abroad or away on a super-secret spy mission that had been extended year after year. They'd talk as if she were still able to offer approval or concerns. Random comments dropped into otherwise normal conversations. Like, *"We bought a new dining table with those clever hidden leaves that Jessica loves."* Or, *"Jessica may think sunflowers are ridiculous plants, but your father has become utterly obsessed with them!"*

It was sad and unsettling. And a little bit infuriating.

I had no intention of sending them a sketch just to hear them say how much Jessica would love it. Or to listen to them wax poetic about how beautiful and wonderful she'd been. I'd heard enough of that at every turn and didn't need to hear more. Besides, though George didn't know it, I had my own imaginary ghost to contend with.

Ed had no opinion on whether I should tell my parents about my drawing. He'd kept tactfully quiet in a way that made me think he couldn't relate to my family drama. He'd likely come from a lovely, supportive family. A family who missed him the way Jessica was missed. Which made any conversation with him on this topic feel stilted and forced. Or maybe it was forced because I knew that I didn't *actually* know anything about his family and that he couldn't *actually* tell me about them.

Because I did know that he wasn't real. Mostly.

It ended up being out of my hands anyway.

About a month before the art show, a local reporter stopped by the Art House to check in with Karin and write a fluff piece about the artists who planned to participate. Apparently, the article happened every year, since Greenville held the area's largest juried show and the Art House was a regular participant. Having rarely read the local paper, I didn't know and scarcely cared. Doris and the others agreed, insisting the article was nothing important.

The reporter showed up one Saturday to capture Karin's soundbites and ask her what it was like to take such an active part in shaping the local art scene. A few of us were there that day, but we kept to ourselves, trying to paint and draw and create as if there wasn't an intruding energy pulling our focus. We tried to be above it.

Eventually, Doris and I retreated to the third floor for coffee and anonymity, but Karin brought the reporter to us. He asked a few simple questions and snapped some pictures before Karin led him back to Becca and Jen's collage. It had taken minutes and seemed like nothing.

After they left, Doris told me Gareth had been the focus of last year's article and probably would be again. Young talent with a bright future. He was becoming well known in local circles and through a larger online audience as well. There would be buyers who came to the art show specifically for him, and he would have his own table as an individual artist. The rest of us planned to submit a few pieces through the Art House collective.

Two weeks after his visit, I'd forgotten about the reporter entirely.

He hadn't forgotten about me.

No one contacted me about the article before it appeared, both online and in print. There was no advance copy and no call to verify my (out of context) quotes. There was only the panicked call from my mother, waking me up before eight in the morning.

"I just don't understand." A common enough refrain from my mother. "Why would you let them bring this all up again? Now when people have finally started to forget? I thought you had more sense than that. But, really! I don't know what you were thinking."

At which point I had to pull myself out of bed to search online and read the article for myself. I was sure she was exaggerating. Maybe the piece had a small mention of Ed, or something about the portrait Karin wanted me to bring to the festival (though I hadn't yet agreed). But there was more than a mention. Much more.

The article's headline yelled across my screen:

Local Artist Exorcises the Ghost of Tragic Murder

Fuck. I skimmed the article with the phone still pressed to my ear, my mother's voice a background of shock and dismay. Butterflies flapped in my stomach as acid rose in my throat. Or I assume they did, in the recreation. The actual memory is a blur, though some sensations stand out. The phone, my landline, was hard plastic digging into my shoulder and ear. The computer screen was bright in the dimly curtained room.

There were pictures in the article. Of course.

There was a shot of me sitting alone on a couch, cradling a coffee cup with barely a smile. (Doris, who had been sitting right next to me when the picture was taken, had been neatly cropped out.) There was a group picture as well. One where Karin had rounded us all up to pose outside the building, and I was squinting into the sun with a slight frown. And then there was a picture of Ed. A nearly finished portrait that I'd thoughtlessly left on my easel when we'd fled for coffee.

Bits of disconnected text jumped out at me. "…*despite having been legally cleared of any wrongdoing…a tragic murder which rocked this suburban town just a few years ago…explores the life-changing effects of tragedy...no stranger to death, having previously lost her sister to cancer…*"

And then the words began to swim, shadowed by questions of where he'd gotten his information and overwhelmed by my mother's unrelenting outrage.

"What does George have to say about this? Do you really think it's fair to him—to your family—to bring this all up again? Publicly? Just when people had stopped talking? Do you know how many of *our* friends are concerned about you? Again? What am I supposed to tell them? How do I explain this? And you didn't even tell me yourself! I had to hear about it from Diane! How does that look?"

In her mind, I *wanted* this attention. She couldn't imagine that an insensitive reporter would sensationalize a fluff piece, or an unscrupulous editor would craft a title for maximum clickbait.

Or maybe she was upset for deeper reasons. Maybe she saw it as some kind of twisted competition. One where I had to choose which experience with death had been most meaningful, and I had better choose my sister over a stranger. Or maybe she didn't want to compare the seediness of Ed's murder to the purity of Jessica's death.

"It's just my art, okay? Tell them that."

"Your art?" Her voice rose a decibel and I heard a deeper murmur in the background. My dad attempting to talk her down. "Are we back to that? Your art? You're not a teenager anymore, young lady. Do you hear me? You are a schoolteacher. Not an *artiste*."

And then there was rustling silence, a struggle, probably my dad's hand over the receiver. The muffle of my parents' whispers about how they should handle this, as if I were still a rebellious teen who needed proper guidance.

Are we back to that? I couldn't remember her saying anything that direct before. Never openly admitting that she didn't approve of my art school or the life I'd tried to lead. Back then, she'd been focused on Jessica, and Jessica had been on my side. After Jessica died, I'd given up drawing, resolving the issue entirely.

I could have told them the rest of it during that phone call. I could have come clean about losing my job and shared that the Art House was meaningful to me. I could have explained that I was hoping to improve and grow as an artist so I could forge a new future—get back on my own abandoned path—whether they thought that was a *real* career or not. But I didn't.

The phone felt hot against my ear and my hand cramped from its tight grip. The pictures on my computer screen bombarded my senses as everything else began to stretch, and bend, and fall away. A calm dropped over me. A detached clarity. I didn't want to be holding the phone anymore, so I clicked it off and left it on the desk. I didn't want to see those pictures anymore, so I closed the browser and walked away.

It was familiar and comforting then. That feeling of being far away. That feeling of being separate. Not just in another place, but in another phase. Out of sync and out of reach.

I'd forgotten how good it felt. After a few weeks of being more present, I'd forgotten how soft and quiet it was when the swirling wind kept everything else away. The only thing missing was a rocks glass for protection. A makeshift Manhattan or a shot of bourbon. Something to hold onto. Something warm. Something to sip at and fuel the haze of not thinking.

But it was early enough that it didn't feel right to get down the bottle.

Another part of me, the same small voice that had always made me wait until after work, was telling me there were other things to do. Other responsibilities. But this time, I didn't know what they were. I didn't have to be at the school. I didn't have to be at the Art House. I could sit in my house and finish off the bourbon. Move on to the vodka. I could drive to a liquor store and buy a bottle of scotch, drink to Ed and to our time together.

But none of that was appealing. Not entirely. None of it felt like *doing* anything. Like *accomplishing* anything. It felt like hiding, when there was something new inside that was driving me toward… What? Toward something. Toward someone, maybe, but not toward anyone I could identify. Not George. Not my parents, not Holly, or Karin, or Gareth, or even Ed.

And, then, in an instant, I knew where I wanted to go.

I knew the one person I wanted to see before I could truly move forward.

Day Fourteen

It takes nearly three hours to drive to New York from our house. I was pretty sure I could make it in closer to two. If I filled up the car before I left and didn't stop for anything. If the weekday rush hour was letting up. I could be there, find Remy, reconnect, and be back before George went to sleep. I'd miss dinner, but that would be okay.

The trip made sense in that moment. Without a doubt. I knew that I needed to go to New York, the same way I'd known that I needed to hang up the phone and shut off the computer. I needed to see Remy, and I needed to be in New York. I wrote a note, packed a bag, grabbed some cash from the box in the kitchen, and I left.

There was no question as to why I was going. It just made sense. Now, looking back, I think maybe I needed to trace my life back to the place where it had diverged and connect to someone who had known me at that point. Someone who could look at me and see if that earlier person still existed, somewhere deep inside.

Or maybe it was something else.

The car needed fuel, so I drove toward town and stopped at the first gas station along the way. I was standing at the pump, ignoring the inane chatter of the video ads playing on the nearby screen, when Becca showed up beside me.

"Hey, you headed to the Art House?"

It took a few blinks to snap out of my hazy thoughts and realize that she was actually standing next to me, with a large tote bag slung over her shoulder and black liner smeared under her eyes. She was just getting off work, she told me, with an eye roll toward the little gas station shop. She was going to walk down the block to the bus stop—unless I happened to be headed her way.

My thoughts were slow in coming together, and I mumbled through some misplaced opening syllables before managing a question of my own.

"I thought you worked at a diner?"

"Yeah, well, I told the skeevy manager to stop grabbing my ass, so he fired it instead. I'm here until I find something better."

I only half-heard her, but something made it through. I heard myself say the first thought that came into my distracted mind.

"I was fired, too."

"Oh, yeah? That sucks."

We nodded together, me waiting for the pump to stop and Becca hitching her stuffed bag higher on her shoulder. It looked heavy and I noticed a second bag weighing down her right arm.

"You always bring that much stuff to work?"

She shrugged it off, but I saw the way she couldn't catch my eye.

"I'm kinda between places now. Had to get the last of my shit out last night. Before my bitch ex-roommate trashed it to make room for her asshole boyfriend."

It made sense, on some kind of *these-things-happen* level, so I nodded again.

I was noticing observations more than meaning in that pleasantly detached state. The morning seemed brighter than it should have been. It was sharp and crisp and hard, despite the heat and humidity that were sure to come later in the day. The flow of gas rushed into the car with a pleasant whoosh and an acrid, but comfortingly familiar smell. A man at the next pump was pacing and texting on his smartphone.

His repetitive motion brought me back from my quiet fog, just a bit. A small step. An inching. And I realized that I hadn't answered Becca about a ride to the Art House.

"I'm going to New York."

"No shit?"

"But I can take you by the Art House first."

"Fuck the Art House, can I come to New York?"

§

We were on the highway before I thought about what I was doing. Or whether I was finally losing what was left of my mind. Jumping in my car and driving to New York wasn't the kind of thing I did. At least, not since I was about 20 years old. And definitely not with a relative stranger.

But that was sort of the point, I think—getting back in touch with that younger self, back on that earlier path—so maybe it wasn't crazy at all. Maybe it was the sanest thing I'd done in years, and all that time in between—all the years of George and marriage and buying a house—was the part of my life that didn't make sense. Maybe that trip was a moment of intense sanity.

Maybe I was being brave. At last.

It's easier to think that way now. To look back and add meaning. But really, it just happened. The way everything was just happening that morning.

Having Becca along gradually broke through the calm. Becca was the way I'd been at that age, young and free and really experiencing life. It was familiar. Natural. But some grown-up part of me cringed at her story of a predator boss and a friend who kicked her out to make room for a boyfriend. It was hard to hear about crappy jobs and run-down apartments and always being uprooted. It was what I'd missed—or thought I'd missed—but it looked a lot less appealing from the outside.

As I listened, and thought more about her situation, part of me wanted to tell her there was a better life without the drama and pain. But was there? Was settling into a steady job, a stable relationship, and a suburban house a better life? Or was it just a safe place to curl up with your disappointments and pretend you never had dreams? Was there any better path in between?

With those questioning thoughts, the world rushed back in. It came with the panicked realization that I was in my car, driving to New York, with someone I barely knew. My heart raced, my hands clutched the wheel, and I fought the urge to turn the car around.

This is crazy, I thought over and over. But maybe it wasn't. I kept driving and didn't tell Becca that I might be losing my mind.

"Have you been to New York before?"

Small talk was better.

"Yeah, a few times. Back when I had a car. And a friend who didn't choose her asshole boyfriend over me. But I sold the car to pay for the Art House and rent and shit, so, yeah, not so much mobile anymore."

We drove without talking then. Listening to the radio and watching the miles fly by. I took deep breaths, blinking at the road and wondering if I was really driving down the highway or whether I was in bed, dreaming this entire day. Becca sat with her feet on the edge of her seat, her arms wrapped around her knees. The silence gave her time to think, and she had to let those thoughts out.

"You know, everything sucks lately. Gaah," she shook her head but couldn't shake her reality. "It just fucking sucks. My bitch roommate, her asshole boyfriend, my fucking pervert ex-boss. My new boss, who is probably a creepy asshole, too. Shit."

This was something I could focus on. Something easier to process than my own possible breakdown.

"What about your parents?"

I felt old as soon as the words were out of my mouth. Like a counselor. (Ugh.) Or a schoolteacher. (Sigh.) But

Becca didn't roll her eyes or groan at the question. She only hesitated a few seconds before answering, though the words came out slowly as she tried to get it right.

"Yeah, my parents are… Well, the thing is, they weren't really interested in being parents. At least not once I stopped being little and cute, you know?"

I knew.

"They had a lot of their own shit going on, and once I hit 18 that was just kinda it. They gave me some cash to get started, and the shitty car that I ended up selling, and said they'd done their job and it was time for me to go be an adult. So, yeah. I don't think they'd be overjoyed to have me turn up on their doorstep now."

"I'm sorry." There wasn't anything else to say.

"Eh, fuck 'em." Becca leaned into the seat and put her feet on the floor. "I've made it this long, I'll work it out. And someday, when I've gotten my shit together and have a family of my own, they're the ones who'll miss out."

I could only nod, trying not to identify too deeply.

"I'm going to have some fucking adorable babies someday—when I'm ready to be a real parent—and they're crazy if they think they can just walk in and be the goddam grandparents and play happy family then."

There wasn't much to say to that either. I drove on, wondering what her parents would do if Becca ever showed up on their doorstep. And how long she'd hold them off if they did want to try again, especially if there was a baby drawing them together. It was hard to imagine parents who wouldn't want to be a part of that. Especially with knowing how much my parents wanted me to give them that life, the grandchildren, now that I was all they had left.

The road hummed beneath the car. Becca was nodding off, and I remembered that she'd probably been up all night, and the day before, so I told her to get some sleep. I could have turned around then, admitted that fleeing was a crazy mistake, but I didn't.

I drove the rest of the way with the radio softly playing and the realities of my own 20s coming back to haunt me.

§

We were almost into the city when my phone rang and woke up Becca. It was Holly calling, but I didn't answer. She'd seen the paper and had texted twice already. Texts I'd ignored. The second had said she was coming over to check on me, and I didn't know how to tell her that I wasn't there. That I'd picked up and run.

I imagined her standing outside my house, cell phone in hand, and I almost picked up. I'd forgotten what it was like to have a friend worry about me and check up if I didn't respond. It made me feel cold and prickly, anxious and unsure, but maybe hopeful, too. Hopeful and vaguely happy in that queasy way of knowing it won't last.

But the tunnel was just ahead, so I let the call go to voicemail and hoped she would understand.

New York is different when driving a car. It's cramped and rushed and slowed and confusing. It's honking horns and yelling cabbies and a GPS recalculating every missed turn. It wasn't *my* New York. I navigated to Greenwich

Village and left the car at the first garage I could find. It must have been nearly one by then, but we'd eaten a box of mini-doughnuts on the way and I didn't want to stop for lunch until we'd made it to see Remy. Until I'd found some solid ground.

"Who is this guy again?"

Becca was all eyes on the train to Midtown, her small-town roots bleeding through her tough exterior. It made me more aware of how brief my time in the city had been. Those days loomed in my memory, but I'd left at the beginning of my second semester and had spent less than six months in New York. Six months that meant more to me than the last ten years of my life, but still only six months.

In Midtown, we climbed the stairs and stepped into a sea of people. The buildings towered, a city bus trundled by, and I was lost. The once familiar block was the same but different. The bookshop where I'd browse on Sunday afternoons was gone, but the glass-fronted diner still glowed with neon lights. Old stone and brick buildings boasted the same scrolled archways and imposing cornices, but they were dwarfed by new skyscrapers that were all glass and chrome. Remy's shop should be just up the street, but it was hard to trust my bearings when I couldn't tell which changes were from rebuilding and which were from my decade of fading memory.

Becca was impatient to get moving, but I needed to just stand for a minute. I needed to take in the rhythm of the city. I'd had a similar moment when we'd first stepped out of the parking garage.

Greenwich Village had been home, however briefly, and it had lived up to my memories. Its warm reds and browns and beiges were still accented with black iron fire escapes and interspersed with shocks of white. Its narrow streets and crowded row homes were still clustered away from wide intersections. There were fewer people on smaller sidewalks and a sky that was closer to the earth. I had pointed out landmarks on our short walk to the subway. Places from my personal history. All of it rushing back while Becca tried to keep up and take in a part of the city she'd never seen.

The energy in Midtown was different than that homey comfort of the Village. Midtown was the New York that had awed and intimidated me all those years ago. It was MoMA and Carnegie Hall, Broadway and Rockefeller Center. We were a few blocks from Central Park, a few blocks from Times Square. This block, slightly removed from the flood of tourists, had the feel of transit. People on their way to somewhere else. To work. To home. Maybe stopping in a shop or grabbing a quick bite, but always ready to get back on the move.

We fell in line with the swarm of people headed toward Central Park, moving like a school of fish toward the next intersection. Taking in the ever-present scaffolding and the sun glinting off glass storefronts. We were almost to Remy's. There was the furniture store, the shoe repair shop, and then we were there. But it wasn't.

I stopped, disrupting the flow and hearing curses behind me. Becca took a few more steps before coming back to look around in confusion.

It was gone. Just gone.

The shop full of art supplies and gentle music. Beatrice's glass-fronted counter and slowly evolving beach. Remy's back workroom. Remy.

Gone.

In its place was a trendy housewares store. Industrial accent pieces, contemporary light fixtures, and minimalist accent furniture. We went in and walked around slowly, not talking. Becca watched me but didn't have to ask. She'd put it together herself.

A well-dressed man, coiffed to match his surroundings, carried a woven bowl full of smooth stone spheres across the room and set it on a chrome table with a subtle flourish and a near-silent sigh. Salesman or performance artist? Probably both. I asked him about Remy's shop, when the store had been sold and where Remy had gone. But I got a blank stare and an indolent shrug in return.

"Honey, please. Do I look like I was here ten years ago?"

And then we were back on the street.

We squinted in the glare as I tried to come to terms with reality. Becca took over then. She led me to the diner, ordered coffee and sandwiches, while I nodded in half-hearted agreement and turned it over in my head.

The shop was gone. Of course, the shop was gone.

I kicked myself for not seeing that coming. For not even questioning, for a moment, whether Remy was still at his shop. Remy was gone. He'd moved on. It was obvious in hindsight. It was the exact thing that would happen. The exact message the universe would send in that moment.

Had I really been stupid enough to think Remy would stay forever, just waiting for my return?

"Don't be so hard on yourself," Ed whispered in my ear, consoling while I nibbled at my club sandwich. I realized that he'd been quiet all day, keeping his distance. Or I'd been keeping him at a distance. *"You never see these things coming until they happen,"* he said softly. *"No one does."*

Then his face was in front of me. Pale, gasping, staring. The combined smells of blood and scotch and his unfamiliar home. The weightless clench of my stomach against the flow of blood that seeped through my sweater. His lips parted, about to speak, and his eyes no longer searching.

I closed my eyes against it and focused on the diner. The neon sign in the window beside me. The vinyl booth beneath my thighs. The toasted sandwich in my hand. Rough and crumbly. The sharp smell of the dill pickle and the jumbled chatter from the other tables.

I opened my eyes to see Becca, sitting across the table and calmly asking the waitress for another soda. Patient and present. Unaware of my quiet panic. Or all too aware and simply giving me space.

Forcing the image of Ed aside, I looked for other memories. Older memories. More helpful-in-this-moment memories. Remy had talked about his family sometimes, in Quebec and in France. No one but Beatrice in New York. He'd sold his own art, his sculptures, but I couldn't remember if he'd mentioned a particular gallery where his work had been shown. At Becca's prodding, I looked him up on my phone but nothing useful turned up. There were a few references to his sculptures and several mentions of his shop. Reviews that were posted at least eight years ago. There was nothing about where he could be now. Nothing about Beatrice.

Becca thought we should make the best of it. Hit some museums, go to a club, do something while we were in the city. She might have been right, but I couldn't move on. I couldn't wake up. The city felt so far from the unchanged world I'd imagined it to be. When I didn't rally, she took another approach, suggesting we ask about Remy in a few more stores on the block. In the stores I remembered and in any that looked like they'd been there a while.

We tried but didn't find much to go on.

The people who remembered Remy's shop couldn't say for sure where he'd gone. He may have left the city. His daughter might still be around. They may have both moved to Quebec. He may have moved to SoHo. Different answers everywhere we went.

They remembered Remy fondly though, with smiles and stories I wasn't in the mood to hear, now that he was gone.

A tiny music shop was our last stop. I left Becca chatting with a tattooed guitar player and stepped outside to make a call. I wanted to get back to Holly, but I needed to talk to George first. I needed to hear his voice. He was still at work, still unaware that I'd left. I'd braced for his voicemail, but it was his voice that picked up. It sounded like he was smiling, happy to hear from me in the middle of what was likely an average, boring day. For a moment,

I wanted to make up a story, hang up and drive like crazy. But there was no way I'd make it home before him now. No way to destroy the note I'd left and pretend like none of this had happened.

"Are you all right?" The pause had given me away. The crack in my voice and the stutter when I tried to talk. Through held-back tears, I told him about the article, my parents, and my ridiculous drive to the city.

We sat together, listening to what I'd said and waiting for him to respond.

"I wish I were there with you," he said at last. "I wish you weren't alone."

He didn't yell. He didn't rant or scold or question. His kindness brought tears and a longing to be back home, with him, not here in this cold and hectic place.

I hadn't told him about running into Becca or bringing her along, and it seemed awkward to add on later. Besides, he'd started talking again before I could explain.

"Stay the night, okay?" His words were gentle. "Go to a hotel, get room service, get some sleep. Take some time to clear your head and come home tomorrow. Okay? You shouldn't drive when you're feeling like this."

Holly wasn't as understanding.

"You're in New York City? You just picked up and drove to New York City?"

I hadn't told her the story in the same way. I'd been more guarded, breezy, trying to keep it light. No tears, no shame. Just a story about how I'd decided to go to New York for a couple of days. On a whim.

"You read the article, right?"

She was piecing it together, feeling me out.

"Yeah."

"I thought you'd be upset by it." It was a statement but also a question. I didn't want to lie, and I didn't want to get into it. I could see Becca through the store window. She was glancing my way and getting bored with the guitar player, who was probably hitting on her.

"Yeah, I was. I am. I mean, I didn't know any of that would be in there, so… yeah."

The silence was strained, making me wish I'd said everything differently.

"I've been calling all day."

"Yeah, I was driving, and then my battery died." The lie slipped out and I cringed at it, knowing she wouldn't believe me.

"I'm glad you're okay," she offered mildly. And then, after an uncomfortable silence, she added more carefully, "Call me when you get back, okay? When you're ready to talk."

A few phone searches and we were soon checking in to a hotel on the Upper East Side. Becca asked why we hadn't headed back to Union Square, where there were plenty of hotels closer to the car. I didn't have an answer. I simply said we'd deal with the car later, once the room was settled, and that this was just where I wanted to stay. That was enough for her, especially once we got off the train and started walking to the hotel. She'd never been this far uptown. Her eyes jumped from building to building, taking in her third new neighborhood of the day, maybe comparing it to the pockets of New York she'd already known.

It was late afternoon by the time we had our room keys. The air buzzed, the way it does in front of closed elevator doors when you're waiting for the ding and the opening. The silence was heavy. For me. I'm not sure that Becca noticed. More people wandered over, carrying travel bags and room keys fresh in their paper enclosures. We had no bags, so I tried to look like we'd been checked in a while, then felt ridiculous for caring what strangers might think.

There were too many of them, gathering with pleasant smiles and courteous nods. I had to get away before the big guy with the messenger bag let loose the small talk that was clearly about to break free. Quickly pulling out one of the room keys, I handed Becca the envelope with the remaining key and said I needed some fresh air. She shrugged, content to check out the room alone. As I slipped away, the crowd moved into the elevator and I heard a deep, friendly voice say, "Nice hotel, eh?"

Outdoors, I stepped closer to the building, avoiding people, and took a few deep breaths. The hotel was in a residential area. Upscale, high-rise condos scattered amid older, shorter buildings that looked like they could be from the 1920s. The Jazz Age. The days of prohibition and lost inhibitions. Stuffy politics and smoky speakeasies. Cold gin and hot piano. Another time that was left in the past.

I could use a gin.

Maybe more than one.

To the right of the hotel, I could have walked down by the East River, maybe watched the hypnotic rhythm of the water passing by while I gathered my thoughts. Instead, I headed left, deeper into the maze of towering glass and weathered brick. I wandered, as if I were aimless, and let the neighborhood unfold around me.

On the next block, an iron gate closed off the open expanse at the back of a four-story middle school. The gate drew my attention, and I stopped to rest my hands on its solid bars. The school was closed for the summer, but I could imagine kids passing through this gate at the beginning and end of each day. Kids older than my students had been. Three to five years older.

Kids who were Mindy's age now.

She'd have just finished sixth grade. No longer the youngest in the middle school. Settling in and moving up. Did her substitute parents, her aunt and uncle, bring her to school each da or did she walk on her own? Did she like her classes? Did she like her teachers?

Catching myself, imagining how it must look to be gripping the bars of a school gate, I let my arms drop by my sides.

"Why are you here?" Ed's voice crept in, prodding for answers. *"Did you really need to see Remy? Were you running to or running away?"*

Ignoring Ed wasn't easy, not once he'd put an idea in my head. He was insistent, and I couldn't lie to him. There would be no point. But wasn't I being honest? Of course, I'd wanted to see Remy.

"Did you?" His voice was firm, but kind. *"Or did you want to imagine another life? What fantasy are you really playing out here?"*

Turning from the gates, trying to shut out Ed's voice, my heart raced at the sight of a family walking toward me. A couple about ten years older than me with a daughter who looked about Mindy's age. The age she'd be now. Same long dark hair. Same slight frame.

But it wasn't Mindy. Of course.

The girl smiled as they passed, lagging a few steps behind. Maybe she was a student here. Maybe she was wondering who I was and why I was hovering outside her school. But she kept walking with her parents and didn't look back. I waited a full ten seconds before following them down the block. Though I told myself I wasn't following them. They were simply walking in the direction I needed to go. But when they turned away from the hotel at the end of the block, I made the turn as well. Why not? It was a nice day. I had time to look around before heading back to the room.

Did they live nearby? Would I if I'd stayed in New York, met someone like George, and started a family? It was a nice neighborhood. Someplace I might have liked to live. If I were raising a family and could afford it. Could I afford it now?

As I strolled behind the family, Ed chimed in.

"And now you're stalking strangers?"

I ignored him, feeling each thud of my footsteps on the wide sidewalk.

The family didn't have far to go. Midway down the short block, they turned into a sushi bar. The father stepped aside to hold the door for his wife and daughter, giving me a friendly smile as I crossed behind. I couldn't go in. I didn't even want to go in.

I kept walking, heading away from the hotel. Just a little bit farther. A few more steps. My heart knocked against my ribs, though I was sure I didn't know why.

At the end of the block, a glass building rose high into the sky. I resisted the urge to look up at its height, but I slowed as I passed the brass sign near the front doors, and

I recognized the name. There was a doorman beyond the glass, talking to an older woman who was carrying a small dog in her arms. My heart hammered as I imagined living in that building. Having a bedroom that overlooked the city, maybe even with a view of the river. Having a family in a place like that, a place so worldly compared to my own suburban town.

Just beyond that luxury building, I came upon the same red brick of the middle school. Its front doors had signs telling visitors to check-in at the security desk, just like our schools back home. The windows in those doors were shot through with safety wire, and it looked dark inside. Empty. But a camera beside the doors kept me moving. Not that there was anything wrong in walking by, but loitering outside a public school wasn't a great idea. Especially after I'd already lingered around back.

I stopped further down the block, catching my breath and getting my bearings. I hadn't walked far or fast, yet I'd broken out in a cold sweat and there was a stitch in my side as if I'd sprinted the whole way.

"What are you really doing here?" Ed whispered.

It was time to go back. Becca was waiting in the room. We still had to go downtown for the car and the bags, then decide what to do for the night. Where to get dinner and much-needed drinks.

"That's it?" Ed sounded surprised. Maybe a little disappointed.

"That's it," I mentally answered. *"You were right. I don't belong here."*

The sky was getting darker. Not from twilight but from thick clouds and the threat of rain. A wind blew through the buildings, bringing a chill to my shaded spot. I rubbed my upper arms and walked back up the block.

Looking ahead, I saw a drug store on the corner, across from the high-rise, and realized we could stop in there for necessities like toothbrushes and toothpaste, if we didn't want to go back for the bags. I didn't know what else to do in this part of the city, but there were restaurants and bars that weren't a half-hour train ride away.

"You're giving up then?"

The question caught me off guard, bringing a mix of confusion and anger.

"You're so close."

His words made me stop again, rubbing my temples as if I could block him out. Or maybe rubbing away whatever blur was making his words so hard to follow. *Giving up on what? Close to what?*

And then I saw him.

He stepped out of the drug store just as the clouds moved on, leaving him bathed in sunlight. He frowned as he squinted up at the glass building.

He couldn't be real.

But he was.

He was there. Right there. Right across the street.

There was no thought as I walked up my own side of the street, glancing across at him without watching where I was walking. Cars passed between us, but it was *him*. It became clearer with each step. As impossible as it could be.

My feet sped, my breath rasped. My heart thumped its way into my throat.

Closer to the corner, opposite from the spot where he stood, I stopped.

I turned. I stared, blinked, and stared again.

And then he looked right into my eyes.

We stood together, locked in place, for just a moment.

His eyes narrowed as if trying to place me.

And then I ran.

§

I half expected him to be outside the hotel when I left with Becca an hour later, but he wasn't. We walked to the subway at an easy stroll, Becca telling a story about her last trip to New York, my eyes scanning each face we passed.

Not him. Not him. Not him.

By the time we were downtown, I'd convinced myself it was all in my imagination. It had to be. The man on the street had been a stranger, and it was the stress of the day that had tricked my mind. Nothing more.

"That wasn't you. Tell me that wasn't you."

I knew it wasn't him.

It couldn't have been Ed Dombrowski, casually walking out of a drug store. Standing on the street corner. Breathing.

I wanted to hear that from Ed himself. Confirmation. But he was silent. Utterly and completely silent. As if he'd never been in my head at all.

At the bar, Becca started another story, skimming the menu and not noticing that I wasn't listening. My mind was busy recreating that moment. Picturing that man on the street, standing in the glare of the sun that had suddenly broken through the clouds. It hadn't been Ed Dombrowski. Obviously. The man was similar, but not the same. Similar features and build. Similar dark hair. But there were many similar men walking around. Tall with dark hair, two eyes, a nose, a mouth.

My tired mind could have imagined any of them to be Ed. I could have imagined him in the bar, across the room or walking in the door. But I didn't. I'd only seen him on that street corner. Which didn't mean anything.

I forced him out of my mind.

Like everything else, the bar wasn't quite the same as I remembered. It had the same dive quality, with smeary tables and worn wooden booths. The hamburgers and fries were still good, and the drinks were still strong. But it was different, too. The music was too loud, and the lights were too bright. The drinkers looked too young to be there, and no one I knew was about to walk through the door.

Half-listening for a sign of Ed, I tried for a distraction, asking Becca question after question. Getting her to tell me more about her life, her dreams, her plans for the future. Waiting for Ed to chime in with wry observations that never came.

"I don't know," Becca sighed into her cocktail—a crazy concoction with ginger and honey, booze, and a sprig of something. "I'm doing this collage thing with Jen, but I'm not as into it anymore. I like to draw, and mix in other media—magazine cut outs, scraps of yarn, whatever—but there's not, like, a future there, you know? Or maybe there is, for some people, but probably not for me."

She took a sip of her drink and I nodded, about to tell her that self-doubt was normal, before she went on to say, "Gareth says they're good, but he would say that." And the look on her face made me realize something I hadn't noticed before.

"You and Gareth are… together?"

"Oh, well, no." She ran a hand through her hair and frowned. "I mean, we were, maybe, but then… Fuck. I don't know."

I asked her what happened, while signaling the waitress for another round.

"Nothing. It's just… He's just so… fucking nice. So fucking normal."

"And the guys you date usually aren't."

"No." Becca's laugh was raw and ugly, but it drew me in. I met her eye, hoping to show that I'd been there. "There was this one guy in particular…" Becca trailed off and I waited until she was ready.

"We were kinda together in high school. And then I moved in with him when my parents kicked me out. Which they didn't like, but why the fuck should they have a say when they didn't want me in their house?

"Anyway, he'd always been… well, I don't know. That kind of controlling guy. You know? The kind who tells you what you want and likes to fuck with your mind and shit." She paused then, showing a trace of fear in her wide eyes. "You know guys like that?"

"Yeah," I nodded, almost reaching for her hand but sensing a nod was enough. I'd known guys like that. I remembered what it was like to be pressed into a wall or pinned to the ground by someone bigger and stronger. Someone who *knew what I really wanted*, despite what I had to say about it. I remembered how it felt to be smaller and weaker. The detachment and the giving up.

The waitress came with more drinks, and I thanked her before taking a large hard swallow. The room was a bit blurry by then, but it hadn't softened enough.

"So, yeah, living with him was a nightmare. But he *was* paying the bills, and it wasn't like I had anywhere else to go, so I stayed for, like, a year. Until I finally saved up enough, and found a roommate, and got out. And it was ugly for a while. After I left. But eventually he gave up."

"And then you met Gareth?"

"Well, like two years and a few assholes later," she shook her head and nudged her drink along the table. "And Gareth was just… different."

The bar was as loud as it had been all night, but the sound seemed to pull back when Becca lifted her eyes to meet mine. We were alone then, letting our locked gaze say all the things that were too hard to say out loud. Feeling our way through the moment.

"George is a nice, normal guy, too. It takes some getting used to."

The tension relaxed then, and Becca's face softened. She told me more about her relationship with Gareth. Their first date, their first kiss. She looked like a different person when she smiled that way. Happier. More confident. But something was keeping them apart.

"It got too serious?" I guessed and got it right.

She leaned in, glass in hand and eyes narrowed.

"He wanted me to meet his fucking parents."

"Ah." Enough said.

"I know, right?" She shook her head, lifting her nearly empty glass and swishing the liquid around the melting ice. "And Gareth's parents? Sure to be super normal and happy and all that shit."

"Maybe," I agreed, knowing that wasn't entirely true.

"No way they'd like me."

"No?" I asked casually. "I think they might."

Becca had the glass halfway to her mouth but paused to consider me.

"Really?"

"Why not? I like you."

She smiled, tossed back the rest of her drink and said something that made me smile in return.

"Yeah, but you aren't normal."

§

"Why did we come here? Today?"

We were several drinks in. The room was bleary, and time had ceased to exist. The waitress had brought us large glasses of water with the basket of mozzarella sticks we were slowly working our way through. Becca took another bite of fried cheese, then added, "I mean, why did you suddenly want to find this art guy?"

She hadn't seen the article.

I brought it up on my phone and passed it over to her, watching her read while I dipped a cheese stick in a dish of sauce and slowly swirled it around. She glanced up at me with wide eyes, but I waved for her to continue reading and looked around the bar at the emptying tables.

It must have been late. I vaguely wondered if we'd be able to get into the garage to get our bags, though I had no intention of driving. Not like this. There was always the drug store near the hotel, if it was open, but the thought of it brought the sobering thought of Ed's look-alike standing outside its doors.

And it had to be a look-alike. Ed could not be there, or anywhere. Not anymore.

I couldn't even find him in my head.

"Wow," Becca gently passed my phone across the table and frowned. "That's some serious shit."

"Yeah," I agreed. "Some serious shit."

"That's why Doris had that look, when she first saw your drawings of that guy. She knew, didn't she?" I nodded. Doris had known. She remembered when it happened and put two and two together after seeing Ed's portrait.

"That must have sucked." Becca looked at me, eyes wide and mouth slightly open. Hunching to lean in a bit. Her voice had come out just above a whisper, trying to be reverent, as she turned over the story she was now picturing in her own mind.

And I laughed. The kind of dry, spontaneous, ridiculous, humorless laugh that goes on too long. Laughing until there were tears in my eyes. A confused look settled across Becca's face, even as her lips stretched into a half-smile, tripped up in worry but eager to join in and ease the tension.

"Yeah," I dabbed my eyes with my fingertips. "Killing a guy really sucked."

Becca's half-smile instantly dropped away.

"You didn't kill him!" She sounded defensive, protective. "It said you were just *there*, and you tried to save him."

"True," I shrugged. "But the woman who did shoot him wouldn't have been there if I hadn't taken her. She wouldn't have gone on her own. And if I hadn't brought her…"

"Bullshit," Becca seemed angry then. Irritated with me. She took a long sip of her water, while I watched the liquid travel up her straw. "You were in the wrong place at the wrong time. You didn't know what would happen."

"Maybe." I wanted to drop the subject. "It's fucked up either way. Ed's dead. I might as well be."

Becca didn't flinch.

"Why?"

She kept her eyes on mine, until I was the one who had to look away.

"Because that day…" I could feel the tears then, the lump rising in my throat and turning my words to a whisper. "That day broke me."

The place was quiet except for a sudden yell from a rowdy group at the bar. Becca reached for my hand.

"You're not broken."

"Really?" It came out more biting than I intended, but I let her hand stay on mine.

"You said yourself that I'm not normal. You could see it, before you even knew why."

Becca brushed the thought off, waving her free hand vaguely and shaking her head.

"That's not broken. That's just… not normal. And normal's not such a great thing anyway." She paused to think about it. "Though you're closer to normal than you think. Like, on the verge of normal, with something just a little off. But off in a good way." She let go of my hand and we drank our water together, quietly regrouping and listening to what she'd said, until she abruptly asked, "Why don't you have any kids?"

"I… uh…"

It was clear the idea had just occurred to her, and she wasn't old enough to realize why that might be a sensitive question. Something I might not want to talk about. If she'd been ten years older, she'd have been wondering if there was a problem and whether she should recommend the fertility doctor she'd heard so much about. And I would have bristled at the subject and felt like she was judging my decisions. But she was only twenty-two and her blunt question had come from simple curiosity.

"I don't know."

It was true, but I strangely wanted to give her a better answer. Was it because of Jessica? Was it because of Ed? Was it because of my shitty opinion of the world around me? Was it because I resented the pressure to conform? But none of that felt right, so maybe *I don't know* was the most honest answer I could give.

"Well, you should." Becca lifted her water, as if in a toast. "Have them, I mean. You would be a fucking awesome mother."

I shook my head, but she insisted.

"You would! You know why? Because you *know*. You know? You know what life—like, real, actual life—is really like."

And I took that as the compliment it was, hoping that it might be a little bit true.

§

Though maybe it wasn't really like that. Maybe that's the conversation I want to remember. Or need to remember. Because, really, that whole night—that whole trip—is just a scattered blur.

Day Sixteen

The nightmares came back that night. Maybe it was sleeping in a strange bed. Maybe it was the booze. They came back in the ususal way. Looping through that day. Flashing through images, more or less in order, and highlighting details that are fuzzier when I'm awake.

The clink of Ed's drink on the glass-topped coffee table. The sound of a truck passing by. The feel of the gun in my clenched grip, and the terror of seeing Ed's face beyond the line of the barrel.

But that isn't right.

The gun wasn't in my hand that day. Sometimes it's hard to keep that straight. To separate what Liz and I have done when we share so much regret.

The nightmares woke me while it was still dark. I stayed in bed, trying to breathe, and listened to Becca's soft, snuffling snores. We'd left the car, and the bags, back in the parking garage. None of that had seemed important at whatever time we'd stumbled out of the bar and made our slow and scary way all the way back to the hotel.

That stupid hotel on the Upper East Side, where I had no reasonable reason to be.

By the time Becca woke up, I'd quietly gone out for some basic toiletries from the corner drug store, buying them with furtive looks for Ed's doppelganger, who—of course—did not appear. I brought them back with coffee and bagels from the hotel's breakfast buffet, and Becca seemed particularly glad for the hot coffee.

"What time is it?"

She tore into a bagel without leaving her bed.

"Almost check-out." My head was lightly spinning, and I desperately wanted to crawl back under the covers, but it was time to head home.

Becca showered before we left, not wanting to waste the opportunity when she wasn't sure where she'd be crashing next. It was an obvious hint, but I bit my tongue. Better to talk to George about that first. A panicked flight was one thing, bringing home a stranger—who he didn't even know was with me—might have been a step too far.

When we got back, I dropped Becca at the Art House but didn't go in with her. She had my cell number and would check in later, once she knew if she could stay with Jen. That gave me time to tell George about the trip, and about Becca's situation, before deciding what I could offer. And what I was willing to offer, in the light of day.

Driving to my own house felt surreal. The streets were exactly as they had been the day before. The neighborhood hadn't morphed into something else while I was away, not the way New York had, but everything felt vaguely foreign.

Not in a bad way. If anything, it was more like noticing everything—really noticing it—for the first time. The clean, tree-lined streets with flower beds blooming in front of welcoming front porches and kids running around at the corner playground. The glimpses of back decks and side patios where neighbors were grilling hamburgers or sipping summer cocktails.

When the garage door opened, George's car was parked inside. That came as a surprise since it was early for him to be home from work. But what surprised me even more, was that seeing his car brought a sense of relief.

He didn't say a word when I walked in. He stood in the hallway near the garage. Waiting. Until I dropped my bag and buried my face in his chest.

His arms were around me in an instant. We were clinging to each other. Wordlessly. Pulling closer. Pressing tighter. Until we were kissing and stroking and undressing. Melting together.

§

Later, entwined and happy, he ran his hand over my hair and down my back as I told him about the pointless trip. He didn't react when I explained about running into Becca and bringing her along. And he didn't react when I told him how the city had changed. But his hand did pause to press gently into the dip on my lower back when I told him how it felt when Remy's shop was simply gone.

"I'm glad you're back home." He spoke softly when I finished. Maybe afraid of saying the wrong thing and scaring me off again. But I told him I was glad to be home, too. And I meant it.

"It was hard to go, but I'm glad I did. It feels…"

"Resolved?" George offered. It seemed like the easiest word, even if it didn't entirely capture my thought.

"I guess. I mean, there are a lot of things, from back then, that have never felt finished."

"And now you have closure."

I hate that concept. I hate the idea that everything can be tied up with a bow. Neat. Clean. Finished. But, in that moment, it felt like there was a little bit of truth in the idea. My mind was quiet. No wind. No storm. No Ed.

"Maybe," I agreed. It didn't feel entirely finished, but maybe that was as close as it would get.

"At the risk of upsetting this really, pretty great moment…" George's caution put me on guard. "Do you think this might be the time to reconsider therapy?"

I wanted to be angry at the suggestion—because that was my typical response—but the feeling never came. Instead, I remembered talking to Becca the night before. I remembered how it had felt to tell someone completely unrelated to the incident about what had happened that day. To tell the story in my own words. Maybe it *was* a good time to talk through whatever I was feeling and maybe it made more sense to do that with an objective professional than with a near stranger in a bar.

George hugged me close when I tentatively agreed and said that my running away was worth it if it would finally get us back on track.

Holly was not as positively inclined.

"You took *who* with you?"

We were in her sunny kitchen again, the day after my return. She was laying out frosting supplies for her next cake, while I sipped tea at my island perch. Kelly was watching a video in the living room, ignoring us both.

"It wasn't planned." I'd already explained about running into Becca, and Holly didn't want to hear it again.

"But who *is* she? Some random girl from an art studio? And you took her on a road trip? Just like that?"

Holly's anger didn't make sense to me. She'd been glad to see me and sat me down to tell her everything. But then she got hung up on a pretty minor part of the story. Why would it matter if Becca was with me? The point was that I'd gone to New York and everything had changed. I'd started to wonder why I was hanging on to that day, instead of leaving it in the past. I'd even started to think it was time to get some help with moving on. Becca being there wasn't important. Except that she'd been someone to talk to. Someone who could just listen and… And then I realized why Holly was mad.

"I didn't choose her." *Over you*, I didn't add. "It wasn't like I was thinking clearly. It just sort of happened."

"You just *happened* to bring a near stranger when you ran away from home? To go on a soul-searching adventure? Interesting."

Holly glared when I said her sarcasm was unnecessary.

"Excuse me," Kelly's small voice interrupted with pointed force. "I am trying to watch my show."

Holly sent her off with a hasty apology and resumed her rant in a quieter tone.

"You're so upset that you can't be bothered to return a text or pick up your phone, but having a road trip buddy? Sure, no problem at all."

"Are you finished?"

I'd gone to Holly hoping to talk about the one thing I hadn't said to anyone else. Not to George or to Becca. I was ready to admit to everything about Ed. To explain how I'd been talking to him in my head and, more importantly, to explain how I'd seen him—or thought I'd seen him—on that street corner in New York. I wanted her to reassure me that I wasn't crazy. Or maybe tell me if I *was* losing my mind. Because if I was going insane, for real, it was the kind of thing I might need to know. But I couldn't even get to that part of the story.

Holly smirked at me and rolled her eyes.

"I'm sorry, am I not reacting properly? What would Becca say if she were here?"

"Okay, now you're being ridiculous."

"And you're spinning out of control."

She was right, of course. And I needed to hear it. But I didn't want to hear it.

I said she was jealous I had anyone else to turn to when she liked being the one with all the answers, the only one who could fix me. And she said skipping town with some troubled kid wasn't helping anything.

It escalated from there. Each of us digging in on our own sides. Bickering like teenagers until Kelly showed up again, waving the remote and complaining that she couldn't hear her show.

"Are you going to be quiet, or do I have to go upstairs?" she asked in an exasperated tone that was a great impression of Holly, or Joe, or some other adult in her life.

"That's okay," I answered before Holly had a chance. "I'm leaving anyway."

And Holly didn't stop me.

§

I'd planned to go to the Art House after seeing Holly, but I couldn't face it after our fight. Part of me wanted to go out of spite. To seek out Becca and Doris and Bill and Gareth. They'd listen and understand. They'd be better friends than Holly was turning out to be. Except… maybe they wouldn't. None of them had called, or texted, or come looking for me. Maybe they didn't want to see me. Maybe they were upset about that article taking the spotlight from their art and from the show they'd been preparing for since long before I'd turned up in their lives. Maybe they even blamed me for Ed's death.

My heart thudded at the thought, making it hard to concentrate on the road. I'd started driving toward Cedar Lake, but my hands wavered on the wheel. My palms felt sweaty, and the day was too bright. With a sharp turn, I headed home. Back toward my neighborhood, past Holly's street and Annemarie's street. Across the highway and down the road from the cul-de-sac where both Beth and Janelle lived in identical split-level houses.

I hadn't heard from any of them either. No one from book club had reached out, other than Holly, and neither had any of my teacher friends. Those distant friends from the school where I'd brought tragedy.

Maybe none of them wanted anything to do with me.

At home, the rooms were shadowed and still. George was back at work. I paced the rooms alone. My palms itched for something. My sketchpad? A pencil? A paintbrush?

I went into the kitchen and poured a bourbon. Not a big glass. Just two fingers. Or maybe three. No ice. No splash of water. No cherries to sweeten and burst. It went down rough, without the benefit of spreading warmth or calming blur.

I'd already felt numb.

Looking at the glass, I could have poured another. There was no one to stop me.

I wanted to be mad at Holly. I wanted to feel bad about upsetting everyone in my life. Everyone except George, who was somehow still there by my side. And I wanted to be upset about that, too. About not being good enough for him. About putting him through hell over and over and still having to look in his eyes and see that he loved me anyway. Somehow.

But I couldn't feel any of that.

And I didn't want another drink.

I rinsed the glass and put it in the dishwasher. Paced around the island. Looked out the window. Tried to gather my thoughts.

It was different now.

Not because I'd run away, and not because I'd come back. It was different because I'd realized that the past—all of my past—was something I carried inside. Privately. Everyone else who knew about it had moved on, letting it become my own personal hell. It was a pain I could cling to and pull out whenever I needed a reason, an excuse, not to move into the future. It was a pain I could use to keep the rest of the world at a distance.

But now it was public knowledge again. On display where other people could question it, making their own judgments and drawing their own conclusions.

It was isolating in a different way. It set me apart in other people's minds. Not just in my own.

It was out of my control.

I hadn't wanted to be exposed in this way. Not by a reporter who wanted to shape the story for his own agenda or by friends who were reminded about something they'd already let go.

Before, I assumed they thought of that day whenever they saw me, now I knew they did.

I could no longer pretend that I'd moved on, too.

And I had tried to move on, before I had resorted to pretending. I'd tried to go back to work as if it hadn't happened. I'd picked up my routine, and welcomed a new class, and kept going to book club. Month after month. Year after year. Until I couldn't. Until Ed's face became so strong, so insistent, that I needed a place to put it. Outside of my mind.

But then... What?

Ed had lived in my canvas and spoken in my mind. He'd let me know him and feel for him. For what he'd lost. For what Mindy had lost.

But where had he gone?

I couldn't hear him anymore. Not since seeing him out on that New York street. Had the bourbon at that bar finally drowned him out? Had the trip let him go? Had I just needed to bring him back to that place? To the place where all of my regrets came together.

Was he really gone?

I went into the study then and dug out my sketch pad. That first one. The mix of high school and Ed and Jessica. The mingling of hopes and regrets and grief.

Opening the pages, they jumped out at me. Their eyes, their smiles, their cheekbones, their jaws. The room spun with them. My hands pulled and tore, page after page ripping from the spiral bind to drop at my feet. The floor filled as I turned in a slow circle. The pages crowded around me, swirling like the storm that was still there, but softer, quieter, dying away in wisps and gasps.

"Where are you?" I yelled into the room. Daring Ed to come back. To speak again. To show that he hadn't actually left. That nothing had really changed.

But there was nothing. No response.

Not a word. Not a sound.

Not a face flickering behind my eyes.

I tore pages until the book was empty. The covers hung from a metal spiral. Limp and useless. Binding nothing. Keeping nothing in. Holding nothing together.

They were around me. Outside of me. But I kept spinning as I looked down at the scattered images. Ed. Jessica. A landscape. A cartoon. A mix of spheres and cubes. Noses, eyes, and mouths floating separate. Disjointed.

The buzzing was there, gentle but distant. Fading.

No Ed. No storm. Nothing to soften the world and keep reality at bay.

On my knees, the floor felt hard under my bones and the room stayed light and sharp. The pages were just pages. Just pictures. Just things I'd created in my mind. Things I was ready to let out and let go.

My breathing was shaky but full.

The clock on the desk came into focus. It was time to clean up. Time to make dinner.

Time to move forward.

Day Seventeen

After New York, everything was different. The Art House could wait until Monday, Becca texted that she had a place to stay, and I wanted to spend some time alone with George. Time to just be a grownup. The kind I'd thought I'd be when I was a kid imagining a future without bedtimes and homework and broccoli five times a week.

We stayed in most of the weekend. Ordering pizza and Thai and sushi. Lounging in bathrobes. Making pancakes and drinking wine. Not looking at anything online or returning calls from my mother. Ignoring all fallout from that stupid article.

That was how it had been before. Back when we were first married and had first moved to the suburbs. Full of hope. Full of excitement about whatever unknowns were around the next corner. There were lazy weekends when we'd blow off the grocery shopping and chores, days when we'd curl up in front of the TV or pull out a deck of cards. That weekend it felt like we could get some of that back. Like we could start over.

That Sunday afternoon, we talked about it. Tentatively. It started as a reflection on how great it had felt to unplug and simply *be* together. George said—after many glasses of wine—that maybe it was better the way we already had it, without pets or kids to get in the way. Surprisingly, I found myself saying the opposite. That maybe adding to the family wouldn't be so bad someday. I don't know if it was the wine. And I don't know if I was talking about a pet or a kid. George never asked.

The Art House was out of my thoughts that weekend. Holly, the reporter, all of it, was out of mind. Out of sight. Out of feeling. It had all ceased to exist, and it was a relief. For the first time in months, I felt no pressure to create. No build-up of energy that needed to be expressed. I could breathe through the day without my palms itching for a pencil. My hands—my heart—felt light. Free.

Maybe that was how it was supposed to be, and I'd gotten it right during those years after art school. Maybe it was better to float along, enjoying and living, without the angst of looking for deeper meaning. I let that idea roll around on Sunday, as George packed up the remaining takeout. I let the feeling of freedom seep through my body as I stretched out in the center of the bed, waiting for him to return.

It was easier that way. Without art. Without creating. Without overthinking.

Until Monday morning.

As George was leaving for work, my ribs felt tight against my heart and shaky lungs. My mouth was dry. My stomach was light and fluid. My palms began to itch, and my fingers gently clutched.

It was time to go back.

I used my key card at the private entrance behind the building. Up the iron spiral staircase and in through the second-floor hallway. Bypassing the store and gallery below where Karin was sure to be waiting behind the counter or straightening one of the displays. It was a privilege of membership. One I hadn't taken advantage of enough.

In the main studio, Becca pieced together her collage, while Doris pinned a fresh sheet of paper to an easel. They didn't see me ease into the room, and I lenjoyed the moment of just watching them work. This was how I had wanted it to be. A space to draw in peace. A place to explore my art without distraction. The reporter had shattered that, but maybe I could get it back. As I stood in the doorway, there was a moment when it seemed like I could go in, set up my easel, and sketch as if nothing had happened. Reset, just as George and I had reset the weekend. Go back to being anonymous and left to myself.

But it was too late for that.

Doris dropped her charcoal when she saw me. There was no time to guess her intent before she rushed over for a long, embarrassing hug. She held my hands in both of hers and looked deep into my eyes while asking how she could help. It was simple but effective, bringing tears that showed how nervous I'd been until that moment of acceptance.

Karin was apologetic, swearing she'd told off the editor of the paper as soon as she'd read it, and Gareth sheepishly offered an ear if I needed to talk. Mysteriously, he then whispered thanks for whatever I'd said to Becca. Even Bill clapped me on the upper arms, saying he'd tell that reporter where to go if he showed up again.

It was sweet and kind and horrible. But lovely most of all.

By the time the sympathies were finished, my heart had been filled with kindness and reassurance. Yet the silence was unnerving as I settled in at an easel. The others resumed their swishing and snipping, and I felt nervous. Something wasn't right. Something was missing.

Someone was missing.

Ed still hadn't returned. Not his voice. Not his face. He didn't whisper encouragement or offer wry observations. There wasn't even a *feeling* of him. He was simply not there, and it felt like a loss. Without his voice and the feel of him, the need to capture his face had also faded. I stood at the easel, amid the comfortable swish and snip of steady work, and realized that I didn't want to draw Ed again. But if I was done drawing Ed, who was next? Holly? Kelly? George? A self-portrait? Did I want to draw a person at all? Maybe a landscape? Or a cityscape? New York? And I stopped that train of thought. Not New York. Then what?

The options were endless, overwhelming me with doubt that I wanted to draw at all, even as my palms tingled with that familiar itch to pick up a pencil. To create. To create something. Anything. To see an image, an important image, emerge from the blank paper.

Where are you?

In that desperate moment, I wanted to hear Ed's voice echo through my head. I missed him. No. It was worse than that. I ached for him. He'd left a hole in me, much like the hole in him. Oozing and gory. But invisible. Still hidden away, despite everyone knowing that I was going through… *something*. They knew I was hurting, but they didn't know I was missing him, too. The Ed that I'd created. The Ed that I'd thought would help me find that *thing*, that elusive something that would elevate my portraits, turning them into real, meaningful art.

Looking around the room, trying to anchor my thoughts, my eyes eventually landed on the large, mullioned windows. The black lines that broke up the world outside, leaving a patchwork of images. An expanse of clouded sky, the lake stretching into the distance, the brick facades of some shops across the way. There were people walking below and standup paddle boards out on the water. Yet I skipped over all of that. My hand began to sketch the window itself. The bold lines of the dark panes. Capturing nothing behind them but focusing on the sharp shadows and the glare of light that gave them texture and depth.

It was something. Maybe nothing special. Nothing important. But it was something tangible. The window gave this room shape and purpose. Maybe this window, like that blue toaster, was more important than I thought.

I sketched through mid-morning, letting the others go up for coffee without me. It was good to be back. Good to feel the pencil in my hand and hear my own swish of graphite against soft paper. It was a window. Just a window.

But I was creating it. Or recreating it. Bringing it into focus. Letting it become a beginning. Of sorts.

When the others came back downstairs, something was different.

It was Doris who led the others over to me, frowning gently and reaching out with her eyes. The local article had been picked up by a larger paper. And then by another. And another. She told me quickly, while the others shifted feet and looked unsure of what to say or do. The story was beginning to spread again, across social media, just as it had four years ago.

As she talked, I looked back at my half-finished sketch of the window. I couldn't remember why I had started drawing it. Was there a purpose? Had I captured anything meaningful at all, or was it just a collection of rectangular lines? I couldn't tell, and it didn't matter. I didn't want to finish it.

I said something to them. I must have. Thanking them for letting me know. Reassuring them that I would be okay. Saying something about being tired and wanting to spend some time back at home, as I packed my bag and forced a smile. They looked at each other, before offering to walk me out, or take me to lunch, or go home with me, and I turned them all down. Insisting, with the smile more firmly in place, that I appreciated their caring but just wanted some time alone.

Which meant no one was with me when I tramped down the inside stairs a few minutes later and saw that the reporter had come back. The same reporter as before.

Frank *Something*. He stood at the counter, talking to Karin, who did not look happy. My feet paused when I saw them together, but I prodded myself forward, avoiding Karin's eyes and deciding not to engage. I thought I was going to make it, past them both and out the door. Until I reached the bottom step and Karin called out to me.

Fuck.

It was tempting to keep going and walk out on them both. But I was better than that. Or was I? My feet slowed again, pausing long enough to be caught.

"Wait up!" Karin outpaced the reporter.

"Someone left this for you," she pressed a small envelope into my hand, adding quickly, "I didn't see him. He left it with Deena while I was upstairs."

And then the reporter was beside us, saying hello and asking if I'd liked the article.

"Frank was just leaving," Karin interjected coldly, but he merely smiled. Oily. Unctuous. Smarmy. Not leaving.

"Passing notes?"

He raised an eyebrow at the card in my hand, and I quickly slipped it into my bag. Karin glared at him, crossing her arms as she said it was time for him to leave.

"An admirer?" He teased, I suppose. Teasing for information if not for a smile.

My face stayed pointed toward Karin as I sighed and closed my eyes in an excessively long blink. I had no idea who would leave a note for me, or what it might say, but my imagination had kicked into overdrive, taking my nervous system with it.

"Okay," Frank held up his fingertips, backing slightly. "Karin tells me you weren't entirely happy with our story." *Our?* The word stuck in my mind. *Our* as in me and him? Or *our* as in him and his crappy local paper?

Whatever he meant, the story he'd written wasn't his and I told him as much before turning to leave. Itching to be back in motion. Desperate to create distance.

"Hold up," Frank stopped me by the door, apologizing but not sincerely. "It's an intriguing story—you have to know that—and yeah, maybe I should have run it by you. But you know what they say, 'it's easier to beg forgiveness than ask permission.' Right?"

"No," I kept walking and when he followed me out onto the sidewalk, I spun to glare at him. There were words bubbling up that needed an outlet. "*I* don't say that," I clarified, louder than intended. "You know who *I* think says that? Predators. Exploiters. Inconsiderate assholes."

He looked at me, then down at my empty hand as if it were still holding the card. There was a small grin on his face and a light in his eyes. Karin had followed us out. She was saying something about harassment and calling the police. He ignored her, staying focused on me alone.

"Who's the letter from?"

"Off the record?"

"Yeah, sure," he grinned more broadly, leaning in.

"Fuck off."

I walked away but could hear his light laughter and Karin's scolding tone. They may have stayed in place or might have been walking behind me. It was hard to tell. My entire body was hot and vibrating while my eyes blinked back a film of tears.

"Come on," he called. "Let me buy you a cup of coffee. Make it up to you."

My feet kept moving and his voice sounded farther away. He had stopped walking. Or my mind was distancing from him. Either way, his voice was fainter with each step. "You know it went viral, right? People love our story. I mean, *your* story, of course. They want to know more…"

I left him behind, though my shaking didn't stop.

At home, the envelope sat on my kitchen island. Innocent and white. Safely concealing whatever was inside. I paced around it, noticing how my name seemed to change from different angles. Sharper, then softer. Spiky, then rounded. The handwriting was slanted. Unfamiliar.

My hands were too empty after I'd set it down. They clutched the air, searching for something solid to grip. Something slick and cold and full of alcohol.

"Just open it already."

Was that Ed's impatient voice or my own? I couldn't tell. Was that a sign that I was better or that I was still falling apart? Still crumbling, bit by bit, step by step, breath by breath? Was the sound of wind and rain beginning to swirl around me?

The envelope was thin. The card inside was thick. An abstract painting was on its front. Something by Pollock maybe. Something appropriately messy. Chaotic and loud. When I opened the card, a glossy picture slid into my hand.

Mindy.

Mindy standing with a group of friends in front of a familiar brick school. Mindy older than I'd known her. Mindy now.

I couldn't look at the picture too closely. Not yet. That would come later. Instead, I set it on the island, took a breath, and concentrated on the handwriting inside the card. It was written in blue ink, with the same slant as my name on the envelope. The words blurred before settling into legible lines:

I saw you in New York, outside her school. We need to talk. Call me.

"You were where?"

I expected anger, but Holly only sounded incredulous. The bourbon shook in my hand. My face felt stiff and sticky with dried tears, and my voice failed. I couldn't say it again without the tears welling up.

"You said you went to New York to find your old mentor? That art shop?"

Holly had been pacing around, but she sank onto the stool next to me. We were in my kitchen this time, sitting at my island while Kelly lounged on a couch in the next room, watching a video on Holly's tablet.

"Remy," I nodded, trying to convince us both.

I *had* gone to New York looking for Remy. As far as I know. But when the time had come to look for a hotel, something else had taken over. Some other half-formed, half-hidden idea that I still didn't entirely understand.

"But you ended up outside of Mindy's school? And outside of her apartment building?"

I think I shrugged then. It was hard to explain the whys and hows of getting there.

"She lives next to the school."

"Uh, huh." Holly reached for my glass and took a quick sip before handing it back. She didn't ask how I knew that.

"What did you plan to say to her."

"There was no plan!"

She listened as I explained it all again. I hadn't planned to see Mindy that day. But we were so close. Just a subway ride from where she lived with her aunt and uncle, who were probably lovely people. Wealthy and educated, if not very good with their social media privacy settings.

"And then you saw Ed's brother...?"

"I didn't know who he was!"

That was the worst part. That maybe I should have known. Should have suspected.

"I just saw someone who looked like... and I thought it was my imagination. From guilt. Or something. I didn't even know he *had* a brother."

"But... Mindy is living with...?"

"No, not with him," Holly's confusion reminded me that there was too much she didn't know.

"Mindy is living with her mother's family," I explained. "Her mother's sister and brother-in-law. Jodi and Harrison Hunt. I don't remember anything coming up about Ed having a brother. Not during the investigation. But I never actually met any of them..."

Holly looked back down at the card, then examined Mindy's picture again. She shook her head slowly.

"Sam Dombrowski." The name sounded ominous. "What do you think he wants?"

I had no idea, but an answer came—in a way—with a curiously timed knock on my front door. Holly came with me, after warning Kelly to stay put. We fully expected it to be Sam himself, or maybe Frank the smarmy reporter. Instead, the peep hole showed an unfamiliar woman standing on the front step. She had short blonde hair and wore a gray sleeveless dress.

She knocked again, and Holly answered.

I cowered behind the cracked door.

"She's not available," Holly told the woman when she asked for me. "Who are you?"

My shaking returned when the woman said she was with the local network news.

"I have a few questions about the Ed Dombrowski case."

"That was four years ago," Holly closed the door, adding, "Move on already."

"But what about Liz Sherman's upcoming hearing?"

Holly paused, and I willed her not to look my way.

"What hearing?"

"She was never tried," the reporter spelled it out slowly, switching to a questioning tone as if testing to see what Holly already knew. "Due to mental incompetence? Her case is being reviewed now? Again? To see whether she should stand trial or be set free?"

I leaned into the door then, feeling my knees buckle as Holly struggled to hold it open against my added weight.

"And who are you?" The reporter finally asked, in a more suspicious tone.

"A friend," Holly muttered, before telling her to go.

"Okay, okay," the woman stepped back to avoid being hit by the closing door, but she managed to hold it open long enough to hand over one of her business cards. "Just pass this on for me, okay?"

"Yeah, sure," Holly answered after the door was closed and locked.

Our eyes met and hers narrowed sharply.

"Did you know about this?"

Day Eighteen

That damn, stupid, idiotic article. I didn't want it to exist, let alone spread virally across mindless, bored, internet readers who were just looking for a distraction from whatever work they were meant to be doing. I wanted to hate that article. I still want to hate that article. It was that article that brought a slew of reporters who all wanted an interview. A statement. A soundbite. They promised to tell my side of the story but really only cared about digging up any scraps of dirt that would fill space and get hits.

I'd been through this before. I'd suffered my unwanted fifteen minutes, and I didn't want to do it again, so I kept them all away. Closing doors and hanging up phones. Refusing to talk to them or read whatever they'd already written. For two days, I didn't read the articles. I didn't watch the news. And I continued to ignore my mother's calls.

But one message had gotten through.

Beatrice.

I'd left my email address for Remy, or for Beatrice, with a few of the friendlier shop owners in New York, but

I hadn't actually expected a response. Or maybe only in my wildest dreams, which lent credence to the feeling that this wasn't really happening. That I was asleep and caught in a dream. Or a nightmare.

Beatrice had heard about the article from the guy at the shoe repair shop. The one who'd brushed me off and barely looked at the post-it I'd left on his counter. Apparently, after seeing my picture in an article, he'd decided to reach out to her. In other words, he hadn't wanted to get involved when I was simply a person asking for help, but once he'd recognized me in the news…

Beatrice said she'd then read the article about me, seen my portrait of Ed, and been *drawn to it*. She remembered me, she said, and she claimed that Remy remembered me, too. *Fondly.* She explained that Remy had retired to Quebec, and she had left the city, too. That city. She'd moved to Philadelphia and opened a small gallery. Something of her own. She asked if I went to Philly often, realizing we were so close now. *Practically neighbors.* She asked me to come in sometime and bring my portfolio.

Because of that damn article.

Maybe someone else would have been happy about that. Grateful. But, in my mind, it ruined everything. The article may have cracked open a door, but it made walking through impossible. Of course, she wanted me when my name was spread across the country by a sensationalist media hungry for clicks, and comments, and reshares. But did that say anything about my effort? About my art?

Or was that the way art always worked?

I tried to set that aside and hang on to the first flush of excitement I'd felt when seeing an email appear with her name on it. I even looked up her gallery online and browsed her sleek, cool website. It appeared to be a small space, but the art she displayed…

It hurt to turn an objective eye on my careful sketches with their meticulous lines and timid wash of colors. It hurt to imagine showing them to Beatrice, only to see her patronizing smile and calculating eyes as she assessed the traffic my name might bring in. My name, not my art.

It hurt, so I left the email unanswered.

§

As the reporters began circling, speculating on Liz's fate and exposing the horror of forensic psychiatric care, I found myself sitting on my couch across from her lawyer and the lead detective from Ed's case. George had summoned them, after reading about the case online, and they'd shown up at the house on a rainy afternoon. Neither had expected the other to be there, and George hadn't warned me that either of them was coming.

I never would have agreed to the meeting, but there we were.

Detective Amy Frye sat in the chair to the left of the fireplace, while the lawyer, Ben Owens, sat to its right. George perched beside me on the couch, where I tried to let him hold my hand. It was an odd gathering and Amy seemed particularly bothered by the arrangement. She stayed though, watching me. Watching everyone. Every cell of my body remembered that look. That unnerving way she took in every expression, every flinch, sigh, cough, and blink. Always watching and assessing. Always judging.

Ben had a lot to say at that meeting. Amy was tight-lipped and white-knuckled.

My own attention was challenged as Ben painted a picture that was hard to hear. Liz was still waiting to be tried, more than three years after the crime, and not in the comfortable psychiatric hospital of my imagination. It was meant to work that way, but it didn't. State forensic hospitals were underfunded and overcrowded, leaving people like Liz—people unfit to stand trial—waiting in prisons for beds to open up. In the years since Ed's death, Liz had been shuffled from prison to prison, briefly getting a bed in one state hospital only to have it close and send her back to another prison where she was held with other criminals, without benefit of trial.

As we sat in my living room, Liz was in one of the state's last two remaining forensic hospitals. She'd been there for a few months, long enough to be assessed and treated (whatever that meant). With beds in high demand, her doctors were claiming success and recommending that she either be tried or released.

"It doesn't make sense," George spoke for us both, while I fought back images of Liz surviving in prison. Liz as I'd last seen her, broken and confused, stuck years in the past and claiming that she'd finally saved her sister. Liz who had turned on me, on my one visit, yelling that I'd betrayed her.

Liz who had been restrained by orderlies when she lunged across the table at me, screaming to know why I hadn't done something to save her.

"If she wasn't sane enough to stand trial, how could they put her in prison?"

"Because state hospitals don't have enough beds," Ben repeated patiently.

"But that can't be legal?" George grasped my limp hand.

"It's legal to be held in prison while waiting for space in a state hospital for ten days, but when there's no place else for people to go, they can end up waiting months. Sometimes, as we've seen with Liz, even longer…"

They faded out then. Or I did. The details of Liz's confinement were more than I could handle. I'd heard enough to know that she'd spent more time in prison than in hospitals, and that the hospitals were struggling to stay open, let alone provide adequate care.

"Is she… better?" was all I wanted to know, and one look at Amy's face canceled out Ben's resounding yes.

"They can't continue to hold her without trial," George insisted, still stuck on what was fair. "But they can't just let her go either."

"It's not a simple case." Amy leaned forward in her seat. "Someone from the District Attorney's office can meet with you to explain it in greater detail."

"And get you on their side," Ben interjected, causing Amy's lips to press into an angry white line.

"There's another hearing on whether she's now fit to stand trial on July 25th," Amy continued as if Ben hadn't spoken. "You aren't required to attend, though if the case does go to trial, you likely will be expected to testify."

"July 25th?" George gripped my hand as I tried to slip it away. "That's a week from Friday. Why are we only hearing about this now?"

Ben and Amy exchanged a brief look, and I finally managed to wriggle my hand free. I crossed my arms over my chest, then uncrossed them, before dropping them by my sides and sliding one hand carefully under each thigh. Our seated tableau branded itself in my mind. The time lengthening and shrinking and falling away.

It should have been me demanding to know why I hadn't been informed sooner. But I didn't feel outrage.

I couldn't look at them. Or at George.

I think I knew what was coming, even when I thought I didn't.

"We *have* been in touch," Amy answered slowly, dropping each word with its maximum weight as I felt George's gaze turn my way. "I reached out myself, as did someone from the District Attorney's office."

George's mouth dropped open, but no words came out. Amy continued in her steely, steady, straightforward voice, though her eyes were kind and gentle. Looking back, it's clear that she understood something that I didn't yet, or that I couldn't yet.

"Your wife was informed months ago."

And the storm came back. Just like that. Not a rustling wind. Not a light rain. A storm that swirled with hurricane force to create a protective wall of blurry, shapeless noise.

George pulled at my hand, lightly shaking my arm. He said my name, over and over, as I nodded, then shook my head. There wasn't an answer I could reasonably give. There was no way to explain that Amy might be right about that. That they might have called and stopped by the school. That they might have tried to outline the situation and what would be expected of me. There was no way to explain that, while also explaining that those things might not have happened at all. That maybe it was all brand-new information to me, even if it did feel eerily familiar.

I sat on that couch, in the eye of the storm, and tried to make sense of what Amy had said. If they had been in touch… If they had told me about Liz's hearing months before…Was that why I'd stopped sleeping and started drinking again? Was that why I'd started drawing Ed?

As I tried to piece it together, I didn't know if the scenes playing through my mind—an ADA visiting my classroom during recess, Amy catching me in the parking lot another day—were memories or imagination.

It was possible, but impossible at the same time. Like so many things seemed to be.

I would remember that, I told myself, over and over. I sat on that couch and told myself that I would *know* if they'd talked to me about the possibility of Liz going to trial, or of her going free. That it was important, memorable information.

But something kept me from contradicting them. Something kept me from admitting that I didn't know whether I'd known about this or not. Maybe because I *should* have known. Because it wasn't the kind of thing a person would just forget.

§

We moved on from there. When it became clear that I wasn't going to admit or deny whatever I may, or may not, have known. There was more to be said, and they weren't going to waste this opportunity. Not when George was there to listen and witness.

"Has Ed's brother contacted you? Sam Dombrowski?"

It was Amy who asked the question. I heard it, clear and direct, through the swirling storm. The question was unexpected, and it created a sort of bridge through the noise. A bridge that might have been rickety and buffeted by wind, but a bridge with handrails I could grip as I inched my way back toward the taut stillness of the living room.

Without turning my head, I felt George's eyes studying my face. Waiting. My relationship with Amy was an uneasy one. If we'd met under different circumstances, maybe at a party or through some work connection, we might have been friends. We were roughly the same age and there was a trace of *something*. Not that she was broken exactly, but that she'd seen enough to understand. To know. But we hadn't met socially. Amy had investigated the murder of the man whose blood had stained my clothes and soaked into my skin. She'd been kind, but quizzical. Firm, but fair. It almost felt as if Amy were on my side at times, though the next minute could change that feeling. I had to remind myself, over and over, that Detective Frye wasn't on anyone's side. She wanted to get to the truth, whatever that truth might be, and I didn't want a softness toward her to lower my guard.

She wasn't Amy to me. She was Detective Frye.

We were not friends. No matter how it felt.

I sat up straighter, lifting my chin.

"I've never met Ed's brother."

"Oh, for fuck's sake," George exhaled sharply, startling me as he stood up and began pacing the room.

Keep it together, my brain was silently begging, but George wasn't looking at me. Or at anyone else. Instead his eyes were on the ceiling. His hands were interlaced at the back of his head, elbows out to the side, as he blinked and frowned and shook his head from side to side.

I'd told him too much. About Sam's card, the picture of Mindy, and the fact that I'd been standing outside Mindy's school in New York. He knew that I couldn't explain why I'd gone there. Even if he didn't know how Ed had taken up residence in my mind. He knew about Sam, and he knew too much.

"George?" Ben and Amy exchanged another look that I tried not to see. I dropped my eyes to the carpet instead, feeling my heart race and wishing again that George had never called them.

George turned back to me, but I didn't look up at him. I could see his feet, out of the corner of my eye, his toes pointing in my direction. He was standing firm, but I was tensed to move. Ready to get ahead of him if I had to. He didn't know where I'd stashed the card from Sam, but it wouldn't take long for him to find it. I would have to be faster. If it came to that.

"Has Sam contacted you?" Amy asked me again, directly, once she'd decided George was waiting on me. That he would continue to wait on me.

I shook my head, just the tiniest movement, before I heard a sharp inhale from George. He was giving me time to talk, but that wouldn't last forever.

"He left a message for me at the Art House," I spoke carefully, knowing that a message could be verbal. "He left his number and asked me to call him. But I haven't."

"I see," Amy paused long enough for me to risk a darting glance. I thought I would see her looking at George, or at Ben, but her eyes were still trained on me. They were kind again. Knowing and encouraging.

"He doesn't want Liz released," Ben chimed in, though that fact wasn't surprising, given that Liz had killed Sam's brother. "He wants her to stand trial, and he's hoping you'll speak out against her."

"She's already given her statement," Amy broke in before turning back to me. "Has he asked you to change your testimony? Has he asked you to say something else about that day?"

"I haven't talked to him."

"It's better that you don't," there was concern in her voice. I think.

"Changing your statement now could be perjury." Ben stood, and George stepped close.

"Are you threatening my wife?"

Amy got between them, insisting that no one was threatening anyone, while I kept my gaze on the ground. Though Ben backed up, his voice was insistent.

"Remember what Liz has been through. Held for going on four years now, without trial. Without being convicted of any crime. Whatever Ed's brother says, however much he's grieving, you know what really happened. You know that Liz was trying to save Mindy."

"Ben." There was a warning in the detective's voice, but Ben ignored her.

"If this goes to trial, they'll try to paint you as another victim of Liz's action. Is that what you want? To be used by the DA to keep a wounded woman in prison?"

"Ben!" Amy barked.

"After she's already suffered and already put in the work to heal?" he rushed on.

"We're done here." Amy decided for us.

I kept my seat while the rest of them moved toward the front door, but Ben turned back from the hall.

"Mindy's aunt and uncle have written a letter in support of Liz's release."

George faced Ben as Amy's eyes rose to the ceiling.

"They claim that Ed was abusing his wife, and she planned to leave him. Before she died in that car accident."

"There's no evidence of that," Amy interrupted valiantly, but her tone was weary, weak.

"Don't talk to Ed's brother, please." Ben's tone made me look up to see the warning in his eyes. "He may be dangerous."

"That's enough." Amy took his arm, guiding Ben toward the door, where he stopped to add a parting shot.

"Mindy's family has a restraining order against him."

"Ben!" They began to argue over what should and shouldn't be said about the case. I closed my eyes, blocking out their voices and the thoughts in my head.

Once they were gone, George began to list all the reasons I shouldn't get involved. I wasn't a mental health professional. Or a lawyer. Or a judge. I needed to put this behind me. Liz's fate wasn't—and shouldn't be—in my hands. I should tell the truth, if subpoenaed, but otherwise keep my distance. Move on.

He agreed that no good could come from meeting with Ed's brother. He said that it sounded like the case went a lot deeper than we knew and that we didn't need to get involved with that. He made a strong case and part of me knew it was good advice.

But I met with Sam two days later.

Day Nineteen

When I got to the restaurant, he was already there, waiting for me. It was beyond unsettling to see a flesh-and -blood person casually wearing Ed's face. They weren't twins, but the similarity was striking. Same basic bone structure. Same eyes and hair. Though there was something thicker about Sam. His features had more weight and his body more brawn. There was the hint of a tattoo on the side of his neck, curling up from the edge of his collar.

We sat, sizing each other up, for what felt like minutes. Neither of us seemed ready to speak. So, we sat. After a while, which may have been just seconds, he thanked me for meeting him and I nodded, still not ready for words. I expected an interrogation. A demand for an explanation. It didn't come. Instead, he looked down at his coffee.

"You know what's going on?" he asked his cup.

I nodded, though he couldn't see me. By the time he looked up I'd stopped nodding, but he seemed to take my silence as an agreement.

"Which side are you on?"

It was easier to breathe when he was talking to his coffee. His eyes—Ed's eyes—were on me and they didn't look like they were going to move away.

His question took me by surprise, though it shouldn't have. Were there sides? I suppose he wanted to know how I felt about Liz. Whether I blamed her or was sympathetic. That seemed reasonable, though I'd never thought of it that way. I'd been too busy blaming myself.

"Why did you go to see Mindy?" He tried a different approach and I turned to look for the waitress, signaling for a cup of coffee. She brought it quickly and offered a lunch menu, which I declined with a forced smile.

We were at the small Italian restaurant at Cedar Lake. The one within sight of the Art House. It had been my idea to meet there. It had seemed safer. A place where we might have talked if I'd just happened to run into him, or if he'd been waiting for me outside of the Art House one day. A place that could look like a chance meeting—if no one checked our phone records.

I thought about this new question, but I didn't have an answer for it either. No one wanted to believe that I hadn't gone to New York to see Mindy. Even though I hadn't actually seen her. No one could understand that I'd been there for another reason, a more personal reason, and that the side trip to Mindy's neighborhood had been a secondary whim.

"So, they got to you?" Sam leaned back in his seat and shook his head at me. "Jodi got to you. She told you her bullshit lies about Ed and you believed them."

"What lies?" They were the first words I could manage, and Sam seemed to take them as an accusation.

"What lies?" He leaned closer, though the restaurant was nearly empty. "All of it. Her whole story. Look, Jodi never liked Ed. She hated him for marrying her little sister. Just because he worked with his hands for a living instead of being some finance prick like her father and her husband. She hated him for taking Ellen out of New York. Whatever she told you was her own bullshit version of the truth, not the actual truth."

He didn't know that I hadn't been inside Mindy's apartment that day. To him, it must have seemed like I was leaving the building after meeting with Jodi—Mindy's aunt—to hear her side of the story. In his mind, that put me on Jodi's side, which reminded me what Ben had said about her.

"Jodi thinks Liz should be released?" It was a question, but Sam seemed to take my words as a statement of fact.

"And what does that tell you?" His fists clenched on the table, while I shook my head and lightly shrugged, unable to answer.

"What did she tell you?" He continued in a lower voice. "About Ed? About Liz?"

"I—" I wanted to tell him that I'd never met Jodi, or her husband, but the words were frozen in my throat.

"Did she tell you that bullshit about Ellen planning to leave Ed? That she was afraid of him? That she was going to take Mindy and run? That same bullshit she fed that guidance counselor?"

"What?" The room began to stretch, even as Sam leaned closer across the table.

"It isn't true." The voice whispered too softly to be recognized. Was it Ed or my own thought? Did it matter?

"It's not true, you know," Sam unknowingly repeated the words in my head. "It was all her bullshit to get Mindy away from Ed. And you know how that turned out."

Sam sat back, drumming his fingers.

I could only stare.

"Did she even tell you that she talked to Liz about Mindy? Before Ed was murdered?"

I shook my head, eyes wide, and something deflated Sam's shoulders.

"Yeah, I guess she wouldn't admit it, even to you," he spoke softly, as if to himself, before turning his attention back to me. "Fine. Then what *did* she tell you?"

I swallowed, steadying myself, and answered honestly.

"Nothing. I never went in the building. I've never met Jodi, or Harrison. I was just in New York, and thinking of Mindy, and wondering how she was, and…"

The surface of my coffee rippled gently. It was a small vibration that drew my attention and, once I saw it, I couldn't look away. I couldn't look back at Sam, who looked too much like his brother. I could only look at the coffee while his words echoed in my head.

Was his story true? Had Jodi told Liz that Ed was abusive? Could she have known what would happen? What Liz would do with that information? She couldn't have. Even if she had wanted Liz on her side. Even if she was hoping to plant the idea… But could Jodi's story actually be true? The Ed I knew wouldn't hurt his wife. The Ed I knew had loved his wife and daughter more than anything in the world. He'd sunk into depression and struggled to go on after his wife's accident. He'd pushed himself to meet me, his daughter's teacher, when he was clearly still grieving. He'd brought his daughter soup and stayed home from work to take care of her when she was sick. He'd… But I couldn't finish the next thought. Because I hadn't known Ed. Not really.

Talk to me, I found my mind looking for Ed as I stared at the coffee. *Tell me what to believe. Who to believe. Where did you go?*

I knew it wasn't real—that the Ed in my mind wasn't real—even when I was actively trying to find his voice, but I had to look for him anyway. I know how that sounds. Like I was crazy. Like I'd lost touch with reality. Maybe I had. I don't know. I only know that as I sat at that table, I had to hear Ed because in that moment I needed him more than I'd ever needed anyone else. Whether he was real or not. I needed him to sort everything out. I needed his voice to help me. To tell me what to think.

The ripples in the coffee became larger. A rattling sound made me notice that my hand was shaking against the ceramic cup, making it tremble in its curved saucer. It hurt to breathe. I raised my eyes and wasn't surprised at the calculating look on Sam's face. At the questions and possibilities floating behind his eyes.

How much time had passed?

Sam didn't ask if I was okay. He didn't ask what I'd been thinking.

"You haven't actually talked to Jodi? Or Harrison? Ever?" My head wobbled cautiously side to side. "Mindy?"

My eyes dropped to the table as I shook my head again. Sam gave a low whistle.

"They haven't tried to get in touch with you at all? They haven't even told you how Mindy's doing? How she's adjusting?"

Part of me agreed with his indignant tone, but the rest of me felt like there was nothing to be upset about. Why *would* they talk to me? They didn't owe me an update on Mindy. They didn't owe me anything.

"They're keeping her away from me, too," Sam added bitterly. "They say I upset her, which is bullshit. I upset *them*, that's who I upset. Not Mindy. I'm still her goddamn uncle, too."

He took a slow breath then, calming himself. Maybe noticing how I'd flinched at his anger. He drained the rest of his coffee and tapped his index finger on the table.

"What about this Liz then? Did you agree with her about Ed? About him being a drunk and a bad parent? Did *you* think he was dangerous to Mindy?"

"I—" My mouth opened, but no sound came out. I wanted to say something, maybe assure him that I didn't know what Liz would do, or say that I hadn't suspected anything, not really, but I'd made the mistake of looking him squarely in the face and the full tension of the meeting swept over me. It was hard to breathe, impossible to speak.

"What are you doing here?" Sam's face but Ed's voice in my head. *"Why are you doing this?"*

"I have to talk to him," I thought-messaged Ed, still unsure if the thoughts were from him or me. *"For you. I have to tell him what happened. Answer his question and help him put the pieces together. Help him the way I couldn't help you."*

As I gathered my words, steadying my breath, the waitress came back to ask if Sam needed a refill. He shook his head, letting his eyes linger on mine. Considering.

"I think we're ready for something stronger." He turned to me. "What do you drink? Bloody Mary? Gin and tonic? Rum and Coke?"

"Bourbon. Neat." It was an automatic answer. Not an order, just an answer to his question. But he turned back to the waitress and ordered two, telling her to make them doubles.

When she was gone, he sighed and nodded slowly.

"All right. Tell me your side. Tell me what happened that day."

§

I don't remember what I told Sam. I wish I could remember, but I don't.

It started slowly, whatever I'd said. It started because I thought he deserved to know how his brother had died. But I also didn't want him to hear *all* the details, because maybe that wasn't good either. Not for him, or for Liz, or for me.

I'm fairly certain that I was careful with my words.

At first.

I stuck to the facts, I think. At least in the beginning. As I sipped that first bourbon, telling myself *Just one drink, for courage.* There was a lot I didn't know about *why* any of it had happened, and it seemed okay to tell him that. It seemed okay to tell him that I didn't know what Liz had planned. Sam probably knew that anyway. It also seemed okay to say I had no idea that Liz had a gun, and it seemed more than okay to express regret. To say that if I could turn back time, I would do something, anything, differently if it would have saved him.

It seemed less okay to tell him the gory details. To talk about Ed's blood and how desperately I'd tried to keep his blood inside his body. But I might have talked about that, too. After the second (or third?) bourbon. There are snippets of memory from that conversation and some of them include blood. Some of them include holding out my hands and asking if he could still see the blood. Some of them include his holding my hands and telling me that it wasn't my fault. That he blamed Liz. And Jodi. But that he didn't blame me.

Whatever I said, I'm sure it seemed right in those moments. Sam had nodded and encouraged and passed me his drinks when mine were gone. He said how much he wanted me on his side—needed me on his side. We talked about Liz, though that's hazy, too. I couldn't blame her entirely, knowing that she hadn't been well, but I couldn't *not* blame her either, knowing that she had pulled the trigger. And Sam understood that, too. He sympathized with me, I think. He said that he needed my help for Liz's sake as well.

To keep her safe, where she belonged. Safe from herself and safe from hurting anyone else.

At least that's the impression I have now. From what little I remember.

§

Sam was going to help me home. He paid the bill, but the waitress stopped us at the door. I think she asked if I was okay and, at the time, I thought I was. I felt perfectly safe. I was with Sam. Ed's brother. Of course, I was safe. How could I not be safe with the man whose brother I'd accidentally helped kill?

There may be a downside to bourbon.

The commotion began when we got outside.

That's a blur, too, but there were suddenly people all around. For a moment, I cringed against Sam, thinking it was more reporters moving in. But then gentle hands separated us, and I looked up to see Annemarie's serious face saying something about getting me home safe. As we walked away, with me leaning heavily into Annemarie's fleshy side, I turned to see Karin arguing with Sam. Doris and Bill stood close by her side. Gareth was a step away, holding his phone to his ear.

Annemarie was not a person I'd expected to see, or wanted to see, that afternoon. I may have even cried when she put me in her car—weak, ugly tears—embarrassed and insisting that I was okay. But she didn't argue, or criticize, or ask questions. She simply made sure my seatbelt was fastened before driving me home.

Life is never simple, but it can be funny. Not in the *ha-ha* sense, but in the *is-this-really-happening* kind of way. It was like that when Annemarie was the one to step in and save me.

She was detached, pragmatic, as she took charge. When we got inside my house, she helped me to the bathroom and waited outside the door. She settled me on the couch with a lap blanket, then started a pot of coffee and brought me a large glass of water while it was brewing. As I sipped, she sat on the ottoman, directly across from me, and very slowly shook her head.

"I'm sorry you're going through this." Her voice had its usual strident tone but was softer around the edges. The judgment she often radiated was replaced with something else. Compassion and understanding on a level I'd never expected from her.

Annemarie brought my coffee when it was ready. She propped me up with some pillows and tucked the blanket around me. I may have dozed off then. A short time later—or what felt like a short time later—there were more voices in the room.

Annemarie returned to tell me she had to go back to work, but Doris and Bill had brought my car home. It was parked in the garage and my keys were in the bowl by the front door. Right where they belonged. Holly was standing beside her and they hugged before Annemarie left, proving that the world is a confusing place.

Day Twenty

The meeting with Sam scared me. It embarrassed me.

Fragments of it came back to me the next day, each bringing a fresh wave of shame. Shame in the things I remembered saying, but also in not remembering what else I may have said. And I'd done it to myself. Drunk enough to lose control of my words, my behavior, and my own memories. There was shame in that, too.

It was hard enough to keep the storm in my head from blowing my memories away, yet there I was, again, fueling the void with the warmth of bourbon. Because sometimes self-medicating is easier than being clearly present with my own thoughts. Unarmed.

I didn't know which was more upsetting: forgetting due to excessive alcohol consumption, like people often do, or forgetting because some trauma-brokenness made me block out whole conversations about Liz's upcoming hearing, the way people—sane people—rarely do.

If I could forget time like that—with or without alcohol—how much control did I actually have over anything? Drunk or sober? How broken was my brain? Was I even safe to navigate my own life? Was I any better, any saner, than Liz?

When I was drinking with Sam, Liz was being held in the forensic ward of a state mental hospital. When I'd been teaching schoolkids and stumbling through my life, she'd been held in prisons, with criminals, despite never having been tried for a crime.

We were both there that day. No jury had heard the facts, and only one of us had been locked up, deemed unfit to stand trial or have a chance at freedom. Because she'd fired the gun, and I'd tried to stop the bleeding. But we'd both been there that day.

After meeting with Sam, I desperately wanted to stay out of it, forget everything, and leave Liz to whatever fate might bring. I wanted to appreciate my freedom and move on before anyone had a chance to take a second look at my involvement. But it was too late for that.

I was already a part of this. Because I was there that day. And because I'd gone to see Sam, telling him things to unburden myself. Making it worse for Liz, in trying to make it better for me.

I remembered things Sam said that afternoon—in fragments—and where I didn't remember his words, his attitude had made an impression. His anger. His thirst for vengeance. All of that rage stated calmly, with the absolute knowledge that he was in the right. That he had the right to ensure his brother's killers were punished.

Killers. Plural.

For Sam, the guilt extended to Ed's sister-in-law, Jodi. He was sure she'd been behind it. That she'd contacted Liz and planted her fears and suspicions. Which was something I'd never considered, and something he couldn't prove, as far as I knew.

But he didn't seem to blame me.

Sam treated me as an ally. A fellow victim. He'd lost his brother because of Liz. I'd become an alcoholic mess who couldn't keep her job, or start a family, or be a healthy, happy part of society, also because of Liz.

I didn't like Sam's view of me. I may have been struggling, but I wasn't a victim. If I had felt like a victim before, I didn't after the shame of that meeting. Each memory of slurring through my story, stumbling through the restaurant, and sprawling into Annemarie's arms bought a keen sense of shame. And responsibility.

Whatever I'd become since the day Ed died, it was my own doing. My own responsibility.

And that's when the new nightmares began.

In my new dreams, I'd been subpoenaed to testify against Liz but decided not to go. I went to the Art House instead, where I stood with my mind empty, unable to find a subject to draw. Ed wouldn't talk to me. Jessica wouldn't talk to me. It was utterly silent. My hands still and my mind as blank as the canvas in front of me.

Then Sam would show up. With a gun.

There was no one to stop him as he'd grab my arm and press the gun into my rib cage. He'd tell me that Liz needed to pay. That I owed it to Ed, and Mindy, and even to myself to see that justice was served. And then he'd walk me to the trial—conveniently close in that dream-travel state—at gunpoint, saying I had to show them what a mess Liz had made of my life.

There were people outside the courthouse, but they didn't notice as he walked me closer to the doors, a gun digging into my side. But somehow, I would get the upper hand. There was a struggle. A reversal. I would find myself holding the gun in my hands. I would see Sam—who looked so much like Ed—standing helpless as my hands shook and my finger twitched against the trigger. The storm would swirl. The air would shake. And if he died, I knew it would be my fault. Again.

The dream repeated whether I was asleep or awake. The picture of aiming a gun at Sam's heart (Ed's heart?) became so insistent I could barely close my eyes without seeing it. Desperate to erase the image, my mind came up with other endings where someone saved Sam from me. Sometimes it was Amy convincing me to give her the gun. Sometimes it was George. Or Holly. Sometimes—often—it was me, turning the gun on myself.

I never pulled the trigger in those dreams, but it always felt like I was on the verge of firing. The imagined feel of the gun in my hands and the vivid pictures in my head made me shake with nausea. It felt too real. It made me question what *had* happened on that day. With Ed. With Liz. Running through those details, again and again, as I always did, trying to sort the nightmares from reality and only getting them more entangled.

I couldn't sleep. I couldn't think. I couldn't stomach the idea of another drink. And I couldn't bring myself to tell anyone what was happening in my stupid, torturous imagination. I didn't understand then how keeping the thoughts secret was giving them power.

If real life was a movie, a Hollywood thriller, then something like that might have played out. A life-or-death confrontation that would finally bring closure. But my life isn't a movie, and I wasn't going to get that kind of dramatic closure. It was going to be worse, out of my control and sadder, though I hadn't known that then.

What I did know was that I felt torn between two sides. Between Sam and Liz. It felt like I was meant to choose, and I didn't want that. I wanted to stay in the middle. Objective. Hearing both sides. And that's why, despite my disastrous meeting with Sam, I went to see Liz.

§

The visit to Liz required permission, and I was surprised at how easily it was given. I assumed they all knew I was going—Amy, the District Attorney's office, Liz's lawyer— yet no one tried to stop me. George knew I was going, too. He wasn't happy about it, but he accepted that it was something I needed to do.

Or maybe he realized that I would do it anyway and was choosing to be relieved that I'd told him before going. Maybe he saw that as progress.

Though the state only had two psychiatric hospitals, the one that held Liz was less than 30 minutes away. I made the drive in silence, needing space to imagine how the meeting would go. But there wasn't enough time. Before I knew it, I was following signs into the parking lot and scanning a cluster of crumbling brick buildings, some thickly covered in creeping vines.

The campus had multiple buildings, though some were abandoned. The forensic area—where criminals were held— was a small part of the hospital, and I felt self-conscious approaching it. I was a visitor, not a patient, but my skin crawled in warning and my feet wanted to run before I was caught and held. I wanted to be back on my couch, safe in the boredom of eating ice cream and watching TV.

I try not to remember the details. The look of the place. The feel of the air. The smell. It's better not to repeat them. Not to make the place too real in my mind. It's enough to say that the hospital was clearly underfunded. It made me sad for the patients who would have nowhere else to go if it closed, and I tried not to imagine the alternatives.

Liz was different than when I last saw her. Her hair was long. Her face was gaunt. Her movements had a disjointed quality. Sharp, yet stuttering. Like a marionette without strings. It's better to forget those details, too.

Liz smiled when she saw me. We sat across a small table, while an orderly—a guard—hovered nearby. Out of hearing but close enough for safety. Liz wasn't in restraints. She was free to slouch in her seat, which she did in a relaxed, easy manner that I couldn't copy.

"You're here," she nodded, keeping that small, enigmatic grin.

"Yes." I didn't know what to say. "How are you?"

She raised an eyebrow, shook her head in grim amusement, and ignored the question.

"It's okay," she encouraged when the silence continued. "Take your time. Not like I'm in a rush to get back."

That made me wonder whether she had anyone, family or friends, people beyond her lawyer, who came to see her. People who might be hoping for her release.

We sat together, in the same assessing silence I'd felt when sitting with Sam. Except this time there was no coffee, and definitely no bourbon, to ease the discomfort.

"I don't know what to say," I confessed, and her lips tightened in a way that betrayed her casual posture.

"You have questions?" she asked warily, and I wasn't sure what she meant.

"Questions?"

Our eyes met, and I realized she was talking about that day.

"I guess." I stuttered into nervous babble, dropping my gaze to my hands. "But that's not why I'm here. Or maybe I don't really know why I'm here. Or what I want."

"I've written you letters."

I looked up sharply.

"I never sent them," she continued flatly. "I didn't think you'd want to hear from me."

Sitting across from her, I could see a little of the Liz I'd known before staring back at me. In some ways, nothing had changed. She was leading the conversation, pulling me in with information that was both tempting and repellant.

"What did they say?" The question came out, even as I wondered if I wanted to know. She seemed to sense that, pausing before she began. I may have nodded, encouraging her, or I may have stayed still as a stone. Either way, she answered in a casual voice.

"They were explanations mostly. Telling you about my childhood. And what happened to me that day, in my mind. It helped to write to you. Helped me sort things out and get back to reality. Especially when I was in—" she interrupted herself, correcting. "When I didn't have regular therapy to keep me grounded.

"You were a kind of imaginary pen pal, I guess. Though I never sent the letters."

I could only stare at her, completely drawn in.

"Tell me."

§

Her story was hard to hear. I thought I knew some of it, after her arrest. She had an abusive father who had ended up in jail. Her mother had died. Her little sister had died, too, and I had the impression her father had killed her. Accidentally, I'd guessed. Maybe with a beating that had gotten out of hand. I figured Liz had blamed herself for not being home when it happened. For not protecting her little sister.

I didn't realize that it could be worse. Much worse.

Liz was nine years old when her mother died, and she was nine years old when her father began pimping her out to his friends, in exchange for money or drugs. She'd wanted

224

to fight back, to make it stop, but the men were bigger and stronger, and she'd been afraid. Her father had promised to leave her little sister, Karly, alone if Liz was a good girl and did what she was told. Karly was four years old.

The first time, Liz didn't know her father had arranged it. She thought she was being left with a babysitter while her dad went to work. But while Karly slept in the next room, the babysitter—her father's friend—held her down and touched her. He did things to her that she didn't understand. Things that hurt and made her cry.

But when she told, her father had a story ready. He always had a story of why she couldn't tell. Why they had no choice. How she had to be good to keep protecting Karly. He said it was her fate, for being pretty like her mother. He said some women were made to be enjoyed by men and those women could use that power to make a fortune. Besides, he said, no one would believe her.

Liz had gone along until she was fifteen, rushing home from school and never going out with friends, always keeping an eye on Karly. Then she had a chance to go on an overnight trip with a school group. Her father said she'd earned a vacation, and he agreed to let Karly stay with a school friend while Liz was out of town. She thought it would be safe. But after she'd left, he met a man who wanted a girl under ten and was willing to pay anything. Liz's father didn't know the man, but he wanted the money. He claimed to not know that the man would be violent, that he'd drug Karly and strangle her. They both claimed it was an accident when Karly died in his bed.

Her father went to jail, and Liz was put into the foster system. She said it was bad at first, but eventually brought her to her real parents, the parents she should have had. A patient couple who took the time to help her get better. Or as better as she could be.

Until Mindy and Ed had brought it all back.

§

Her story, told in calm composure, was hard to believe, yet shockingly, horribly real. How do you respond to a story like that? I listened, feeling the horror shift my face in ways I couldn't control. My gut twisted. A lump formed in my throat. Her words were clear, her body was held in careful stillness, but I knew her interior world was anything but calm while laying out those ugly facts.

"A jury will understand," I found myself reassuring her. "If it comes to that. A jury will see what you've been through, the nightmare you've endured, and they'll have to understand why your mind—" I stumbled. "Why you couldn't— Why it happened."

"Because it was inevitable, right? Because he twisted me into such a monster that I was sure to snap someday?" Liz's words had a dangerous edge and I shifted in my seat, glancing at the guard who may have been too far away to hear much of our conversation. Liz paused, took a deep breath, and returned to her previous calm.

"It explains why I brought a gun to his house," she agreed. "Why I wanted to be prepared for whatever we might find."

Her voice dropped a bit lower, her words clearly intended for me alone.

"But it doesn't quite explain why I pulled the trigger. Does it?"

"Well, I—" Liz was waiting for something from me, but I didn't know what.

"I spent a long time trying to figure that one out," she continued. "Months. Years. I knew why I brought the gun, but I didn't know why I shot him."

"Well, you thought—"

"Oh," she interrupted, and a sarcastic gleam came into her eyes. "You know what I was thinking that day?"

There was fear in my face then. I could feel it pushing my initial pity out of the way. I shook my head, taking back whatever I'd been about to say.

"Well, I've had more than enough time to figure it out. Not much else to do, except think and figure things out. And I'm finally feeling better. So better that I now remember what I was really thinking, and what really happened that day."

I may have asked, encouraging Liz to tell me. Or I may have pulled back, not wanting to know. Both feelings were true. The wanting, and not wanting, to know what she thought happened in those moments before she shot Ed. A familiar conflict.

Before she told me, Liz's lips stretched into a different kind of smile. One that sent a chill down my spine. I took a breath, trying to recapture the compassion I'd felt for her just a few minutes earlier.

"See, the thing is..." She leaned in just enough to make a point but not enough to worry the guard. "That may have been my gun, but I didn't go there alone."

I can still see her face—the coldness, the restrained anger—when she said those words. I can still feel my palms sweat and my throat go dry as she went on.

"We're the only ones who really know what happened in those last seconds. I only brought the gun to keep him at a distance while we made sure Mindy was safe. I never planned to shoot him. Yet he was shot."

The whine of the fluorescent bulbs overhead became louder, shifting into the sound of wind. Of rain. My vision began to pull back, making it seem like Liz was sitting at the far end of a long tunnel.

"What are you—? You shot him."

The words wobbled out of me, barely a whisper. Or maybe they were a shout, though there was no reaction from the guard.

"I never touched that gun," I reminded her. "Your prints were the only ones on it."

"True," Liz nodded thoughtfuly. "But it wouldn't take much to make me accidentally shoot. A bump on the arm. A clumsy attempt to take the gun away."

I was instantly back in that moment. The one right before the gun went off. That freeze frame where my memory always caught, and I could never quite remember. The moment where I felt like it had become my fault. Was that it? Had I tried to take the gun? Had I reached out? Bumped her? Accidentally made the gun go off?

I sat on that metal chair, no longer aware of Liz sitting across from me as the memory replayed behind my eyes. It flowed by, frame-by-frame, but that key moment was still fuzzy. There was no clarification either way. Nothing to tell me if she was lying.

And then a voice came to me.

"It doesn't matter." It was Ed. Not real-life Ed, but the Ed that I'd been missing. The Ed who had been my friend and helped me begin processing the emotions I'd packed away after that awful day.

"It wouldn't matter if you bumped her arm," the voice went on. *"It wouldn't matter if the gun went off while you were trying to take it away. Liz brought the gun. Liz fired it. Liz wanted him dead. Anything else is just her excuse, just her twisted way of not taking responsibility.*

"It was not your fault."

The storm receded, and I stared Liz down. Matching her cold gaze with one of my own.

"I came here to check on you," I told her. "To see if you were better. And I *wanted* you to be better. I wanted you to be healed, and healthy, and ready to start over with a new life. But you're not. You had a horrific childhood, if that story is true, but—"

"If it's true?" Liz began to raise her voice. "If? *If?*"

The guard stepped closer, saying it was time to wrap up our visit.

"Fine, forget it!" Liz shouted as she jumped to her feet. The guard was beside her immediately, a restraining hand on her arm.

"I made it up, okay? Is that what you want to hear? Does that make you feel better? Except I didn't, or did I? You'll never know, and you'll always wonder. You'll die wondering. You don't get my truth! You don't deserve my truth! None of you deserve my truth!"

A second guard came in to hold her other arm. A third woman followed, wielding a syringe. I stepped back, pressed against the far wall, and watched in silent shock.

"All you teachers," Liz raged. "All those years! You all see the signs and look right through them. None of you were ever brave enough to get involved. To step in. No one stepped in to help me. No one! Well *I* stepped in! I did something about it! I saved her! This time I saved her!"

Her screams faded into hazy slurs as the drug caused her to slump between the guards. Or orderlies. Whatever they were called in a place like that. The woman who held the empty syringe looked at me then and told me it was time to go. But I'd already figured that out.

Day Twenty-One

Amy was in the parking lot when I went out to my car. I'd stopped in the ladies' room to catch my breath and settle my nerves before the drive home, but I was still shaking when she startled me by the building entrance.

She'd been inside. She knew about Liz's outburst. Maybe she'd seen it for herself, over the monitors that must have shown video of that room. She was watching me. *Detective Frye* was watching me.

"It's not your fault."

I walked past her.

"I understand why you needed to see her."

I slowed down.

"And why you needed to see Sam."

I stopped walking.

"None of this is your fault."

I wanted to turn around then. I wanted to ask her why she thought it was so hard for me to stay away, since she claimed to have such insight. I also wanted to ask if the story Liz had told me about her childhood had been true, and if I might have done something, said something, that made Liz pull that trigger.

But I didn't.

Ed's voice—*my Ed's* voice—repeated the same message. *"It was not your fault."*

We stood in the quiet parking lot. I heard the crunch of Amy's feet shifting on loose gravel and let my eyes drift over the cars. Something had changed. The voice in my head wasn't Ed. Not any version of him. Ed Dombrowski had never been in my head, and I would never know what he thought, or whether he blamed me.

In the far corner of the parking lot, I saw a familiar man hunched behind the wheel of a brown sedan that appeared to have New York plates. *Sam.*

He was watching me, too.

"He followed you here," Amy's voice came from close behind me. "He tried to follow you in but was stopped by security. Caused a bit of a scene before being escorted out. But you didn't tell him you were coming here, did you?"

I looked away from Sam's car and shook my head.

"Megan?"

That's all she said. My name. In her reassuring tone.

And something clicked. She wasn't my friend, but she wasn't my enemy. She was reaching out. Offering support. The way Holly had. The way George always had. Maybe it wasn't weakness to respond. To meet her halfway.

When I turned around, she was waiting patiently, but I don't think much time had passed. There was one thing I wanted to know.

"Did Ed's sister-in-law talk to Liz? Before?"

Amy frowned, glancing toward Sam's car as if to check that he hadn't moved.

"Did Liz tell you that?"

"No."

"Sam then?"

I nodded, and she shook her head faintly.

"Megan, there's something I have to say to you, and I want you to hear me out. Okay?"

"Okay." I braced myself, ready to be let in.

"This doesn't involve you."

Her words didn't register at first. Was it another way of saying that I wasn't to blame? Did she want to emphasize that before telling me whatever she was about to tell me? But then she made her message clear.

"I know how that day, how Ed's death, has deeply affected you." Amy's words were carefully chosen. "It was traumatic, and it would be traumatic for anyone, but the reasons behind it, and the case around it, has nothing to do with you. You were pulled into a nightmare where you didn't belong."

Maybe she saw something change in my expression because she stepped a bit closer, adding, "You were an important part of that day. You tried to save him. You comforted him and kept him from dying alone. But you didn't belong there, and you don't belong here now."

"But…" I couldn't argue. She was right.

What was I doing there? Why was I putting myself back in the center of it?

Did I want attention? Was my mother right? No, it couldn't be that.

"Your testimony about that day might be needed in the future," Amy went on. "But you don't have to be involved in the rest of this. You can walk away. Go on with your life. Be Megan Avery the schoolteacher, or Megan Avery the artist. Just be something more than Megan Avery the witness. Don't throw your life away over someone else's crime."

§

I thought about that mother-daughter duo on my way home. The ones who were at the craft store, buying yarn. I wondered how they were doing and whether the mother had made progress on that gift. I remembered what she'd said, *"Let's see if I live long enough to finish the damn thing."* And I thought about the way she'd said it, not snide or joking, and without a trace of self-pity. It was a statement of fact, acknowledging that we all get closer to death with each passing day.

I hadn't heard a response from the daughter, and I doubt she'd given one. Maybe she'd rolled her eyes or shaken her head. Maybe it was a comment she'd heard from her mother before and knew she would hear again.

Despite their shopping frustration, I bet they have a pretty good relationship.

As I thought about that knitting mother, I wondered if I'd live long enough to be that nonchalant about my own impending death. There were times when I almost felt that way. Times when death seemed like a good break, a place to finally rest after so much upset. But then I'd remember that death wasn't a break. That death was final and there was no coming back. And that made death less appealing.

I didn't feel finished. Not yet. Even if I wasn't sure what I should be doing or where I really belonged.

Liz hadn't seemed finished either.

I'd stopped thinking about mothers and daughters by the time I got home. Which made it somewhat ironic to see a familiar car parked in my driveway. Another unexpected car with out-of-state plates, this time from Florida.

I didn't see anyone in the car, or on the porch, but when I pressed the door opener, I saw George's car parked in the garage. Parked on my side because their car was blocking his usual spot. I parked behind his car and shut off the engine, closing my eyes and resting my forehead on the steering wheel. When I looked up, their car was still beside me, its white paint reflecting the blindingly bright sun. It was really there.

George met me in the front hall where he swore he hadn't known they were coming and said they'd called him when they couldn't reach me. I fished my phone from the bottom of my bag to see several missed calls and a slew of unread texts. My phone had been on silent, and I'd forgotten to check it in my rush to drive home.

"How was the visit?" George whispered, his hand gently rubbing my arm.

I could hear my parents talking to each other in the kitchen. Their words were indistinct, but their voices were unmistakable. My mother was doing most of the talking.

"Not now." I closed my eyes again, this time massaging my fingertips into my forehead.

"That bad?"

I could only nod.

"Say a quick hello and you can slip upstairs," George suggested. "We'll say you have a headache, and I'll send them back to their hotel until dinner."

"Do they know where I was?" He shook his head, and I nodded. "Why are they here?"

He hesitated.

"Never mind." I waved the question away, knowing he was the wrong one to ask.

They greeted me with hugs and smiles, as if their visit had been mutually planned. There were coffee cups set around the table, surrounding a store-bought strudel they'd likely brought as a gift.

"Are you surprised?" My mother laughed, while my dad had the decency to look worried about my reaction.

"What are you doing here?"

"Oh, Megan Leigh, is that how you're going to be?" She rolled her eyes and began cutting the strudel. "Where are your dessert plates?"

"I said we should have told you we were coming." My dad shook his head but kept smiling, as if my annoyance was an old family joke. "I said you wouldn't want a surprise."

"Oh, people love surprises," my mother insisted, implying that any upset I might feel in their showing up on my doorstep, entirely unannounced, was a failing on my part alone.

George gave me a supportive look, a warning look, before stepping in with a stack of small blue plates. My dad took a seat at the table. There was the sound of steam escaping from the coffee maker as it bubbled to a stop. No one seemed to notice that I hadn't moved.

"What are you doing here?"

They all turned to look at me.

My mother sighed.

"Isn't this where we should be? With that hearing on Friday?"

Her lips were pinched in distaste. She didn't want to be dealing with this, but she was ready to make a show of support. For her friends. For the press. And maybe that wasn't entirely fair. Maybe she also wanted to be there for me. Because she wanted to be a good mother and thought that being here was what a good mother would do.

"I don't know if I'm going to that." I glanced at George, wishing we could have talked about this alone.

"Oh." She seemed almost disappointed before brushing away whatever thought had drifted through her mind. "That's probably best. But if you do, how would it look if your family wasn't there with you?"

"I don't think anyone would notice. Or care."

"You know," she sighed, ignoring my response as she brought the coffee pot and a metal trivet over to the table and started dishing cut slices of strudel onto each plate. "Our visit wouldn't have been a surprise if you'd answered your phone or returned any of my calls.

"Now come join us for coffee."

I wanted to refuse or simply turn and walk away. Instead, I crossed the room and took a seat next to George. I passively accepted a plate and felt George's hand rest gently on my thigh.

It was raspberry strudel. The kind I'd always asked for on holidays and special occasions. My favorite. The sugary smell of it eased some of the tension in my shoulders, and my mouth watered at the sight of the thick, white icing. Was it that easy? Did I just need raspberry strudel to wash everything else away?

I wanted to enjoy that small treat, if only for a few minutes, but my fork only picked at the crumbling dessert. The idea of pleasantly eating strudel while my parents prattled on with their small talk seemed absurd, and its sweet smell became nauseating.

My phone vibrated in my pocket. It was a text from Holly asking if I was home yet. I quickly texted back, *"Yes, but came home to surprise visit from parents!?! Ugh."*

"We didn't want to put you out," my mother eyed my phone but kept talking between dainty bites. "I mean, since I couldn't get in touch with you to make plans, so we're staying at a hotel. Diane and Steve would have put us up, but I'm sure they assumed we'd be staying with you."

"Your parents?!? Wtf?" Holly's response made me smile.

"It's nice to see that you do know *how* to use your phone," my mother interjected sarcastically. "When you want to, that is."

"Caroline," my dad put a restraining hand over hers, then began talking about the new variety of tomatoes he was now growing in their garden. George responded politely, and I ignored them all.

"*I know, right?!*" I went back to texting, shielding the phone below the tabletop and getting a teenage thrill from my minor rebellion.

"*Ugh. The last thing you need! What happened with Liz?*"

"*It was bad. Really bad.*" George kicked my foot, and I rolled my eyes. "*Text more later, once parents are gone. Ugh. Can't believe they're here!*"

"Really, Megan?" My mother broke into Dad's story. "Do you need to be texting someone now? When we just got here?"

"I have some things to take care of." I matched her icy tone. "It's not like I *knew* you were coming."

My phone dinged as a new text came in.

"*Ditch them with George and come here. I have cake!*"

I flipped my phone face down, suppressing a laugh as my mother's frown deepened.

"What's so funny?" She pressed. "Something you want to share with the rest of us?"

"Fine." I could see George shake his head tightly, but I'd had enough.

"I went to see Liz today."

My mother stared at me, fork midway to mouth. George set down his coffee.

"At the state hospital," I clarified needlessly.

"That's not funny." Her fork clattered to her plate.

"No, it wasn't. In fact, it didn't go well. At all."

My father leaned back in his chair.

George pivoted to face me, trying to capture my full attention. Ignoring my parents.

"Are you okay?" His voice was soft. His hands reached for mine, before he thought better of it.

"Well…" I nudged my plate away and turned to answer him in an oddly bright, brittle voice. "Liz told me about her horrific childhood. And she thinks I was the one who made her shoot Ed. She says I bumped her arm, or tried to take her gun, making it accidentally go off. Because she was only there to scare him, not shoot him, so it had to be me who made it happen. Obviously.

"And then she had to be sedated. So, I left."

I crossed the kitchen to look out the back window. George followed, positioning himself between me and my parents, but otherwise simply standing close, silently letting me know he was there for whatever I might need.

"That's ridiculous!" My mother's chair scraped back and her voice rose in anger. "No one would believe that story. No one would believe that crazy woman over you! Matthew, tell her that's ridiculous."

My dad cleared his throat, and it sounded like he'd kept his seat. When he spoke, his words were slow and filled with heavy deliberation.

"Well, I'm not a lawyer, but I think Liz would still be legally responsible for whatever happened, since she's the one who brought the gun."

"Matthew!" My mother sounded exasperated. "Your daughter did not do anything to make that gun go off!" She pleaded with me then, as I kept looking out the window.

"Tell your father that that woman is lying. Tell him that that woman, that Liz, shot that gun all on her own!"

"Caroline, please." George's gentle tone had enough authority to quiet my parents. He placed his hands on my shoulders and suggested that I needed some rest after an emotional morning. He steered me to the living room couch, then went back to quietly consult with my parents before ushering them toward the front door.

They stopped briefly in the living room doorway where my dad told me to get some rest and my mother assured me they'd be back for dinner.

"And we want to spend some time with you tomorrow," she added. "We want to go see that Art House place and see what you've been drawing."

Something vulnerable in her voice caught my attention. When I turned toward them, I saw their arms were linked. She was nervous, and he was hopeful. I nodded and agreed to see them at dinner, after I'd had some time to rest.

Once they were gone, George brought in a plate with a thick slab of strudel and two forks. We curled into the couch and ate, leaning against each other and savoring the sugary sweetness of the icing against the tartness of the raspberry filling.

Then I told him everything Liz had said—and everything Amy had said—while he stroked my back and dried my tears.

Day Twenty-Two

Holly and I had a longer text exchange after George had gone to bed, typing from the chat app on my laptop late into the night. Something about that process—the typing of a conversation—made it easier to hash and rehash whatever I was thinking. Or feeling. I knew it was Holly on the other end, sending back questions and suggestions, but it was different than talking in person. There was no eye contact. No body language or tone of voice. Without all of that, conversations can be harder to interpret. Or easier? Harder to get her intentions right. Easier to hear what I wanted.

It felt a lot like talking to Ed in my mind.

I told Holly what Liz had shared about her childhood trauma. If we were talking in person, it might have ended there. Over text, I shared how small I'd felt in comparison. How trivial my trauma seemed when stacked side-by-side. I may have watched my sister wither away… I may have watched a man die from a gunshot wound… And both of those experiences were bad. Traumatic even. Both had affected me. Bruised me. But Liz…?

Liz had been betrayed. She had been physically and emotionally abused, manipulated, raped. Not once, not twice. But for years. Repeatedly. While she was young and vulnerable. She'd lost her childhood, her adolescence, and her ability to trust. She'd lost her mother. She'd lost her sister. She'd missed out on ever having a father, because the father she was born to had been a monster.

It was too much to comprehend, let alone survive. And it hurt to make comparisons.

How had I spent months—years—feeling sorry for myself? How had I fallen apart over tragedies that weren't nearly as bad? Traumas I had merely witnessed?

A trauma where I didn't even belong.

I spilled all of those thoughts into that late-night chat. Typing it out while sipping bourbon and hating myself for needing the booze, even as I poured a second drink.

But Holly was having none of it.

"It's not a competition," she typed. *"Her life was fucked up. That sucks. But it doesn't minimize your trauma. It doesn't change your pain."*

I struggled with that idea at the time, though I wanted to believe her. I was drowning in the guilt of not being able to handle my own pain more successfully. I felt weak and selfish. Self-indulgent and entitled. Who was I to let my own pain, my own storm, wipe out any recognition of what others, like Liz, were experiencing?

And I felt like a hypocrite, because I was still doing it. With every feeling, I was still focusing on my own reaction to Liz's story. On my own guilt, and shame, and weakness.

"But Amy was right. It doesn't even involve me."

I typed a recap of our conversation outside the hospital, feeling hot tears begin to fall.

"Why do I keep hanging on? Why did I go to New York? Or to see Sam? Or to see Liz? Why can't I let it go?!?"

There was a delay then. A long wait while dancing dots told me Holly was typing and pausing, maybe erasing and retyping. I finished my drink, forcing myself not to pour a third.

"I think there's a line," Holly's text began. *"I think you're involved and not involved. And it's totally normal to want answers and to feel part of it, after what you went through… I mean, *I* want answers and I wasn't there at all. But she's also right that you should stop where you are. You were already dragged in enough. Don't let them—Sam or Liz—or anyone drag you in more."*

I knew she was right. Even then. But stepping back, letting go, felt like losing something.

"You have so many other things," Holly kept typing. *"Friends and George and art. Maybe a whole new career. So much else to focus on in your own life."*

"My parents," I added, dreading tomorrow.

"Ha! Yeah, them too."

I put the cap back on the bourbon, feeling the cork press firmly against its glass neck.

"See? You don't need Liz and Sam and their crazy in your life," Holly texted again. *"You've got enough crazy with your mother in town! ;-)"*

I laughed. Too tired to think about it anymore.

Instead, I told Holly how I'd been roped into bringing my parents to the Art House beefore meeting George for lunch. She offered to meet us, too, adding that Kelly would be an adorable little distraction. She was right, though I winced at the thought of Kelly. She was so young, so unaware of the evil in the world. I wanted her to stay that way, never knowing the torture that Liz—that Karly—had known. Never even knowing that it *could* happen. And then I saw how that was part of the problem. Too many sheltered people content to live their lives without ever getting involved.

Like Liz had said.

§

My parents had come to town to support me. I kept telling myself that, though it didn't feel like support. To me, their visit was one more responsibility I didn't have the capacity to handle.

They wanted to spend the day together. Start with breakfast, visit the Art House, maybe shop a bit at Cedar Lake before lunch. I wanted them to go back in Florida.

I compromised, no breakfast but I'd take them to the Art House before lunch. I wished it wasn't a compromise. I wanted us to have a relationship where bringing them to the Art House would be fun for me, something to share and bond over. But we didn't.

In the morning, George opted to take the day off work. I nearly said he didn't have to do that. Instead, I said I was grateful to have him with me. And the words felt right.

We arrived at Cedar Lake mid-morning, my parents complaining about the heat and humidity, despite being here from Florida. The parking lot was full for a Thursday, and a bustle of workers were setting up for a weekend festival. Booths were being erected along the sidewalks, obscuring the street art and local storefronts. We had to walk around a tall ladder where two men were installing a sound system, and a woman with a stroller nearly ran us into the bushes while trying to wrangle her two older kids.

"It's not usually like this," I offered weakly, making space for my parents to walk ahead.

"Hmmm," my mother pulled her purse close. "A bit old and shabby, but I guess that's what they call *charm* these days. With the *hipsters* and all that."

I kept quiet as we navigated our way to the Art House. Until my mother noticed the Italian restaurant where I'd met Sam less than a week before.

"Oh, I remember that place! We went there for lunch years ago, when you first moved here! Remember? No, wait, you were both at work, and we were out with Diane and Steve that day. Let's go there for lunch!"

"No," I answered shortly, still trekking forward.

Sidestepping whatever else I might say, George began making other suggestions. Suggestions they shot down one after another.

"How about Mexican?" (Too spicy.)

"Asahi has amazing dragon rolls." (We don't eat sushi.)

"There's a great bistro around the corner." (But this is right here!)

George finally told them that Italian was too heavy for lunch, which made my mother scoff at our trendy ideas about healthy eating.

"Tada!" I broke in with an elaborate gesture toward the building at the end of the pier.

"This is it?" My dad adjusted his glasses, peering at a wooden sign that spelled out *The Art House* in large green letters. He let his eyes climb the building, squinting into the sun, before saying, "Nice windows."

"Charming," my mothered offered flatly.

Inside, Karin introduced herself and led them around the gallery and shop. George and I hung back, watching them, though it was his first time there, too.

"I wish I'd brought you here sooner," I told him, not having to add *without my parents.*

"I'm here now." George snaked his arm around my back, his hand resting on my hip as I leaned into him. I let Benjamin Stolarz' mural wait for a better day, wanting to take him upstairs while my parents were busy. But they caught up, and we went up together.

Doris and Bill were in the main studio, along with a woman I hadn't met who was painting at one of the front easels. I'd warned my parents not to disturb the artists, but Bill came over with a booming hello and Doris followed quickly behind, wiping her hands on a smock and gushing words of welcome. Karin must have spread the news of our planned visit. Luckily, the woman up front was wearing earbuds and didn't seem bothered by the commotion.

So far, so good.

With my parents occupied, I walked George a few steps away and quietly pointed out the easel where I usually worked. I showed him my view of the lake, sectioned neatly by the black window frames. He stood close and bent to kiss my temple, one arm encircling my waist. It was one of our good moments, and I tried to focus on that.

When we reluctantly turned back, my dad was talking with both Bill and Doris, while my mother looked around the room with the same pinched expression she'd worn outside. Imagining the studio through her eyes, I saw the paint-spattered tabletops, the peeling woodwork, and the dingy patches on the off-white walls. The low cabinets were made of rough plywood and secured with metal hasps and padlocks, very much like the handmade cubbies upstairs. To me it was perfect, to her it was… what?

I asked my parents to wait there, while I brought George to fetch some of my work from my locker upstairs. They could have come up with us, but I didn't want my mother's eyes judging our cozy lounge space. Doris offered to show them the jewelry and ceramics studios, and we hurried off before anyone could object.

As we climbed the stairs, I began to realize how very much I wanted George to see the space where I'd drank coffee, and laughed, and talked art, and made new friends. The place that had become a home away from home.

We stopped near the top of the stairs, and I turned, one step higher, pausing at his eye level. There was happiness in his eyes. Love, affection. Despite my parents and the legal mess that might be coming. Despite everything. George was happy to be there with me. Happy to finally be asked in, and I don't know why I'd made him wait so long.

I kissed him, there on the stairs. Not a light peck, but a long, tender kiss. Leaning into him as he leaned into me, trusting that we'd balance each other out, that together we'd keep from toppling backward. As that kiss deepened, I felt one of his hands grab the handrail, holding us upright, and his other arm pull me closer. My hands went to the walls, pressing for support, even as I let my body melt into him.

We were breathless when we parted. Faces inches apart. I pulled back, just enough to catch my balance. He let go of my waist, brushing a lock of hair off my face. We smiled, touched foreheads, and sighed. Then resumed the climb without another word. Ready to move forward.

I didn't know Becca and Gareth were already up there.

"Just come home with me, please."

Gareth's voice shattered the spell that had sprung up between us. Across the room, Becca was trying to stuff her two large bags into her art cubby.

"I can't." She was snappish, agitated. "Just let it go."

We stood at the top of the stairs, caught in an awkward stay-or-go moment. And then Gareth caught sight of us.

"Hey," I waved weakly, seeing his cheeks flush.

"Hey."

Becca glanced our way, too, then scowled and went back to wedging the bags into a space where they clearly would not fit.

"This is George," I gestured his way, ignoring the situation. Gareth came over, self-consciously running his fingers through his shaggy hair before offering one hand in greeting.

"Can you talk to her?" Gareth looked tired, as if this conversation had been going on for days.

"She doesn't need talking to," Becca grunted while tucking the loose folds of one bag into the crammed locker. There were bits of photographs, colored paper, and art supplies strewn all over the floor. Items she must have pulled out of her locker in an attempt to make space. Her other bag slouched amid the mess.

I smiled an apology at George, considering our options. My art was in a locker on the other side of Becca's mess. I could wade past, ignoring their argument, fish out a sketch pad, and maybe a canvas or two, to carry back downstairs. It was awkward, but possible. If I wanted to stick to my original plan and not get involved.

Ignoring our interruption, Becca and Gareth had resumed their battle, caught up in a fight about the fight instead of discussing the real problem. She raged that he was condescending, and she could speak for herself. He fumed, claiming he would love for her to speak up, instead being pissed when he couldn't read her mind.

Their complaints were getting louder, yet through the din, I could hear my parents nearing the bottom of the stairs. My mother using her gracious hostess voice, and my dad laughing at something she'd said. They were putting on a show for Doris and Bill, and whoever else was within earshot.

George and I were caught in the middle.

As we stood in that shrinking middle ground, my head and heart began to pound. I felt like a weather map from the nightly news, where the chilly front of my parents' approach threatened to collide with the heat of Gareth and Becca's argument. Here at the nexus, the storm in me began to swirl. George began to fade as I felt my attention pulling inward, escaping the way I often did.

And then Becca threw a pot of rubber cement.

The plastic jar whizzed across the room, past Gareth's head, where it smacked into a wall and fell to the floor with a thud. Gareth froze. Becca froze.

I thundered across the room, stepping right between them. Getting involved.

"All right, that's it!" I was back in my classroom, breaking up bickering children, and I fleetingly wondered if anyone ever grew out of childish tantrums. Or maybe I'm only thinking that now. Looking back.

They glared at each other. They glared at me. George glanced down the stairs and flashed me a look of warning. My parents were getting closer. Probably chatting at the bottom of the stairs, expecting our return any moment. George waved that it was okay and went back downstairs, heading them off.

"Somebody talk," I clenched my jaw, reclaiming my teacher voice. My authority.

"I thought we were moving forward." Gareth spoke to me but looked at Becca. "I thought we were past this."

"Too vague," I cut him off, turning back to Becca. "You want to try?"

She stared at her feet, lightly kicking a pair of scissors. And then it dawned on me.

"Is this about meeting his parents? Still?"

They both spoke up, ready to set the record straight.

A lot had happened since my road trip with Becca. She'd met Gareth parents. They'd liked her, and she'd liked them. They'd gotten along so well that they'd invited her to stay with them while looking for a new place. But Becca was afraid to accept.

As I listened, a voice whispered that this wasn't my fight. I didn't belong anywhere near it. I had my own problems. I was pushing past my bounds, again. It would be better to follow George downstairs and tell my parents they could see my art another day. I could say there was a couple arguing upstairs, and they'd understand. They'd shake their heads over the public display and walk away to keep from getting tangled up in someone else's mess.

But then I remembered what Liz had said: *No one was brave enough to step in. No one was willing to help.* I remembered Gareth showing me his beautiful painting and saying I reminded him of the mother who'd died when he was young. I remembered Becca, sitting in that New York diner, telling me I would be a good mother someday because I understood what life was really like.

Maybe this didn't involve me, but maybe that was okay. Because maybe this was a time when I could help.

"Seriously?" I sighed at Becca, ready to dole out some tough love. "Your *problem* is that you met some nice people who want to help you out? Wow. How terrible for you."

"It's not that—" Becca tried to correct me, but I wouldn't give her the chance.

"Not that simple," I finished for her, but then took a deep breath and dropped the sarcasm. "Look, I get that this is weird for you, and you don't want to screw it up. You aren't used to having parent figures who care enough to put your needs first. I get that.

"Trust me, I get that. But Gareth's parents aren't your parents. They're making an effort, and maybe you could at least try to meet them halfway?"

"I guess," Becca bit her lip, ripping into a chapped area. "Maybe."

"And you," I wasn't letting Gareth off the hook either. "I'm assuming you know about Becca's parents. Yes? Okay, then maybe you could make an effort to understand why this is hard for her?

"Staying with your family might go well, but it might not—no matter how much you want it to work. And Becca hasn't had a lot of experience with things going well, so you have to decide if you can handle that. Because you'll have to be reassuring about all of this. Not just once, but many, many times."

"I can do that," Gareth reached for Becca and she stepped closer, taking his hand.

It might have been a success if I'd stopped there, but I didn't. I was too full of myself. Too high on the success of finally doing something right. I'd taken a chance, connected, and helped. I kept talking, sharing a deeper thought without thinking it through.

"This parent stuff is never easy," I went on, letting the words just fall out. "Look at me. My parents have had no interest in me for years, but when my name gets splashed around the news, they show up on my doorstep without warning. Now I have to deal with them because they've decided to pretend we're a close family.

"Like I don't have enough to worry about without having to entertain two people who have become virtual strangers, but who still insist I treat them like actual, involved parents."

Which is, of course, when I realized that George had not been able to keep my parents downstairs. As if my life were a TV drama, they'd gotten tired of waiting and had pressed past him, climbing the stairs just in time to hear what I really thought about their visit.

Day Twenty-Three

It wasn't that bad, as far as betrayals go. It was an awkward family misstep. You argue, you clear the air, you apologize, and you move on. It happens that way—in families I've watched on TV and in movies, but we weren't that kind of family. Despite everything we'd been through with Jessica—or maybe because of it—we didn't have a dynamic that let us speak our minds. I know *I* didn't. I was too busy trying to be the good daughter. Maybe still trying to make up for what they'd lost and still trying to fill Jessica's perfect shoes.

The look on my mother's face—and on my father's face—made their pain slice through me like a knife.

It wasn't a small betrayal. It was bad. Really bad.

"Now you've done it." My own thought. I brushed the judgment aside and followed them down the stairs and out of the building, calling for them to wait, to hear me out. George tried to slow me down, saying that maybe they needed a minute alone. Maybe we all needed a minute to think. I didn't want to hear that.

We faced off outside, on the sidewalk in front of the Art House.

"Look, I'm sorry." My regret was real, but even I could hear that I was holding back some other feeling. Something sharper.

"For saying it or that we heard you say it?" My mother waved her hand quickly, wiping her own question away. "Never mind. It doesn't matter. You've always pushed us away, but I thought you'd have better manners than to bad mouth us to other people."

My dad stepped in, putting his hands on her shoulders but, for once, not telling her to hold back or soften. Not making an effort to smooth the situation.

His silence hurt more than her words.

Their expressions of sadness and disappointment made me bite back my anger, replacing it with rationalizations.

They'd come here to support me. They were doing what good parents would do. Yet that didn't feel right. There was something off, something empty. As my rationalizations failed, I felt myself pull farther back. My mind ready to let the storm protect me until the pain had passed.

But the wind didn't come.

There was no rainstorm in my head. No hurricane of white noise.

We stood on the sidewalk, and I felt bad for hurting them, after they'd come here for me. Until that voice—that voice that was me, not Ed—slipped in a single, stark thought:

"But they weren't invited."

As I stood there, sorting through my guilt, the thought repeated. *They weren't invited. They weren't invited.* And then the words came out.

"You weren't invited."

The disappointment faded, as confused anger spread over my mother's face.

"Excuse me?" She shook off dad's hands and stood taller, stepping toward me.

I couldn't look at my father.

"You weren't invited."

It might not have been the right thing to say, but it's what I wanted to say. With a deep breath, I let go of what I should or shouldn't say next. I listened to the words that already existed in my head and gave them voice.

"I know you think you *should* be here. That it's the *right* way to help, but it isn't right for me."

I gathered my courage and felt a heat beginning to rise inside, something stronger, steadier than the storm. It was different than the bravado I'd felt when stepping between Gareth and Becca. It was shakier but becoming more insistent. More confident.

"We don't have that kind of relationship," I told them. "No, hear me out. We haven't built the kind of relationship where we open up about these things. About the big, real, messy things. And we can't suddenly have that kind of relationship now. You can't suddenly show up and be here for me, when you haven't been a part of this. When all you've done is make me feel like I'm not handling any of this the *right* way. The way you think you would."

Holly arrived then, with Kelly in tow. I saw them step in from the periphery, dressed in coordinated sundresses and wearing large, rounded sunglasses. Holly pushed hers onto her head, looking between us, lips parted to speak, but I saw George shake his head her way, holding her off.

"Who do you think you are, young lady?" My mother stood taller, ignoring the people around her. "To talk to us that way? To talk to *me* that way? I gave birth to you. We fed and clothed you. We put up with your wild teenage years. Your leaving us, and leaving Jessica, to run off to New York. And then to marry her—" She cut herself off, still having her limits. "Well. Just who do you think you are?"

And I knew.

"I'm me." I answered with my arms held wide. "I'm Megan Avery. And I'm more than the daughter you raised or the sister I lost. I'm all those things, and I'm everything I've ever been through. And I'm not perfect."

She took a half-step back, cringing away, but I wasn't done yet.

"Do you want to know why we can't go to that Italian place?" I gestured widely, feeling a lightness spread through me. "Because I was drunk off my ass there just last week. Before noon. I was day drinking with Ed's brother, because of the pain. Because it hurts so much that I can't talk about it, can't think about it, without something to ease the pain. Even a little.

"And I was drunk. Embarrassingly, falling down drunk in a way that makes me not want to show my face there again. Not anytime soon."

"Well, I—" My mother's mouth opened, looking for her own words but not finding any.

"And I was fired! Over a month ago!" I ranted on. Unleashing it all. "This isn't just my usual summer off. I don't have a job to go back to in the fall. And I haven't even been looking for one.

"I was fired because I'm losing my fucking mind. This isn't a thing from the past that a reporter stirred up. This is something I've never gotten over and—"

There were tears burning my eyes and rolling down my cheeks. I was choking up. Choking on the words. But I didn't let myself stop. Maybe we *could be* one of those families who shared their pain.

"And Ed died. Right here." I held up my arms. "Right beneath these hands."

"Enough!" My mother hurried close then, slapping my hands down by my sides in one swift gesture. "You are making a scene."

I glanced around, seeing the workmen, the shoppers, the strangers, who had turned our way. Some continued to watch. Some quickly averted their eyes. I couldn't see George, who was standing close by my side, but I could see Holly, whose eyes were cheering me on.

"You need to get ahold of yourself. Right. Now."

My mother's words were a hiss through clenched teeth. She was close to my face. Closer than she'd been since I was very young. But I'd been holding in too much for too long. Maybe I needed to make a scene.

"No," I shook my head defiantly.

Her eyes widened and her lips narrowed as her face filled my vision. We were both breathing short and fast.

"This is me. This is what I'm going through."

It was her turn to shake her head, tight little jerks of refusal.

Annemarie's face flashed through my mind then. Annemarie—of all people—propping up my drunken stagger and getting me home safe. Without a word of judgment.

"If you're here to support me, *really* support me, then you need to see the mess I actually am. You have to see when I'm falling apart and just… stay here. Stay next to me."

She shrank back, pulling away from my emotion. Her eyes went cold.

"There are… *professionals*… who can help with that sort of thing. And if you need help paying for—"

"No!" I stepped in, closing the small distance she'd created, for a moment feeling hopeful that I could make her understand. "I don't need money. I don't even need you to put me back together. I just need you to see the mess and… and just *be here*."

She stumbled in her rush to back away, and I watched my father step in to steady her. They stood together, one blank-eyed, mortified statue. A study in stoicism. Or in terror.

"This has been an upsetting ordeal." My dad's voice was calm when I wanted it to rage. I wanted to see sadness, anger, something. Anything other than the mask of uncomfortable patience that had slid over his face.

His tone had its desired effect on my mother. She stood a little steadier, closed her eyes, and took a deep, sobering breath.

"Perhaps we should go back to the hotel and try again at dinner. Once you've had some time to collect yourself. We can get ourselves there."

I'm sure she meant it as a reconciliation. As a way to move past the uncomfortableness of my ill-mannered outburst. But with that cold, controlled tone, it was the harshest thing she could have said.

Or so I thought.

As I stood there, vulnerable, emotionally bleeding from their indifference, my parents turned their backs to walk back toward the parking lot. Or maybe to the Italian restaurant, where they'd eat lunch without me, then call a car to get them back to the hotel.

But then my mother caught sight of Holly and Kelly, watching us.

Holly looked stunned, but it was Kelly who must have caught my mother's eye. Kelly wasn't paying attention to any of us. She was fiddling with two small blooms that she'd picked from the flowering urn on the sidewalk behind her. Her sunglasses hung from her ears, with the lenses just below her chin. She swayed forward and back, probably to some nursery song that only she could hear, while twining the stems together.

Whatever she saw in Kelly's innocent play made my mother stop and turn back. She pulled her arm free, leaving my dad's side to rapidly cross back to me. I'm not sure if anyone else heard her fierce whisper. It was pitched low, for my ears alone.

"I hope you get this need for attention under control before you have children of your own. You have no idea the strength it takes—the sacrifices you make—to be a good parent."

She spun around, hurried to take my father's arm, and walked away without ever looking back.

§

George, Holly, and I stood rooted in place as we watched my parents go. Kelly flittered over to the flowerpot to pluck another prize.

Holly was the first to look my way, breaking the spell. In an instant, she was by my side, wrapping me in a hug while George half-patted and half-rubbed my back. I didn't see if they'd gone into the restaurant or continued on to the parking lot, but my parents were gone by the time Holly let go.

Holly and George were full of encouragement, praising me for speaking up. For sharing how I felt. I could only nod, feeling suddenly tired and hungrier than I'd realized. Kelly lit up when George asked if she'd like Mexican for lunch, and Holly suggested a pitcher of sangria. I tried to manage a smile.

We walked across the plaza toward a family-owned Mexican restaurant at the far end. A cozy place that Holly said served the best *sopa de lima* she'd had since our Cancun graduation trip. I was gently swept along, caught up in

George and Holly's light chatter, while my entire body—my mind, my heart—felt drained by the confrontation with my parents.

I had nothing left to feel when Amy stepped into our path. She didn't belong there, but there she was. Detective Frye. A grim set to her jaw. A hardness in her eyes.

"Megan." Amy swallowed, darting a cautious glance toward Kelly. "There's something I have to tell you."

Day Twenty-Four

They had found Liz that morning. The day after my visit. Though Amy swore the timing wasn't related. Or—if it was—that it still wasn't my fault. She said that this had been a long time coming. That it wasn't because of anything I'd said or done.

Everyone told me that. It was one of the first things they'd say after hearing of Liz's suicide. *It isn't your fault.* It was her decision. It was her mental illness. It was the trauma of her childhood. It was the system that had left her languishing in jail without a trial. They all seemed sure I would blame myself. But I didn't.

That might seem surprising.

It came as a surprise to me.

After years of blaming myself for Ed's death, I expected that guilt to simply extend, encompassing Liz as well. But something else happened instead. I continued to feel nothing.

No guilt. No nausea. No wind. No storm.

Nothing.

I stayed as empty as I'd felt in those moments before Amy showed up with her news. Those moments after the scene with my mother.

Maybe I'd I hit my limit. Maybe I'd I hit a place where I couldn't take on one more bit of guilt, or shame, or unbidden responsibility.

Or maybe I was beginning to accept that Liz's story wasn't my story.

I've spent twenty-four days writing in this journal. Writing something that is meant to be a story of sorts. A record of my crazy summer—*the summer of my crazy?*— or whatever this is. But when I look back over what I've written, it's such a mess. Such a scatter. There are threads. Bits of myself. Facets of myself. Of my story. Not quite pulling together, but maybe beginning to take shape.

And a story needs an end of sorts. An end of a chapter, at least. This chapter of my summer. An end before the beginning of something new.

§

I went back to our house after talking to Amy. On what would have been the day before Liz's hearing. The day after my visit. I went back with George, Holly, and Kelly. Others showed up as well. Later. As word spread. Some friends from book club. Some friends from the Art House.

My parents came back, brushing away any attempts to mention our earlier conflict. It didn't matter anymore, they said, and I didn't bother arguing the point.

I was busy feeling nothing.

That afternoon was directed toward me—everyone gathering to be there for me—but I don't remember what was said or what anyone did. There was wine and some kind of food. There were speculations and reassurances. There were distracting anecdotes and offers of whatever I might need. Everything that goes with a time when people feel they should be together, despite there being nothing they can really do.

It was only later, when everyone was gone and George was asleep, when I began to feel *something* creeping in. It wasn't the heavy guilt that would have felt familiar. It was more of a general, hazy regret and sadness for the situation. For Liz. For Ed and Mindy. For Sam. For everyone who had been touched by everything that had happened.

It was a vaguely familiar feeling, too, but still different. Somehow.

Whatever it was, it was enough to keep me awake. Enough to get me out of bed, leaving George in a deep and weighty sleep.

The bottle of bourbon was closer to empty than full. I brought it with me into the den, along with a generous glass. I'd skipped the cherries, the vermouth, the bitters. I sat in the dark, sipping. Alone in the room where I'd first drawn Ed's sad eyes.

I don't know that I really wanted that drink, but maybe I wanted a recreation. Drinking alone, in the dimness of the den. Recreating what the environment had been when Ed had first appeared. Was I trying to bring him back? Was I inviting Liz in?

I knew it wouldn't work. The spell had already been broken somehow. I suppose by accepting that Ed was only my voice in my head. It had never been him. Never would be him. Just as I'd never hear Liz, or Jessica, in anything more than my imagination.

So I left my sketchpad closed. And I drank.

I drank out of habit or as a way to cling to the numbness. To the nothing.

There's not much I remember from that night. The night Liz died. The first night without her in the world. But there are moments, details that come back.

The glass was empty, but the bottle wasn't when I left the house.

The bottle was with me when I parked my car at the Art House.

The bottle stayed in my hand as I climbed the iron staircase at the back of building.

It cradled in my arm as I swiped the key card that would let me in after hours.

There were sketches of Ed in my third-floor cubby, but I don't think I touched them. When I made my way back to the main studio, I had a blank canvas pinned to my favorite easel and a pencil in my hand.

The bottle was still with me.

The studio would have been silent. The sky dark beyond the looming windows. No moon dand only a scattering of stars. I remember a streetlight just beyond the large window spreading an eerie glow across the room as I stared at the blank canvas.

It was Liz's turn to be captured on my page. Another death added to my tally. Another death that wasn't quite my fault, even if I had been there—or nearly there—when it happened. Always part of it, if not directly. Not the one to pull the trigger, or tie the noose, or infect with cancer. But still there. Still a witness. Still standing just to the left of death.

My hand shook. My body shook. My lines were jagged as the canvas shifted in front of me and the floor swayed below. The feeling of nothing was competing with that something else—the regret, the sadness. Liz's face flashed in and out of my mind. The tip of my pencil cracked against the paper, and I watched a bit of soft lead fall to the ground. In great detail. In slow motion.

I reached for the bottle, seeing it blurred on the side table, and then it was gone.

The bottle sailed across the room as if launched on its own and shattered into the lower edge of that huge, mullioned window.

There was a *crack!* as two small, rectangular panes splintered and fell from their metal frames. And then it was silent again.

I remember standing then, my eyelids fluttering, while I waited for something to happen. A siren. A rush of feet. Something. But everything remained quiet. Stepping closer, over the broken glass, I saw the gaps where two panes of glass had been. I saw a series of fissures that had spread in some of the surrounding panes.

Everything became clear.

I'd broken the window.

There was no question, no ambiguity. The window was broken, and I had done it. I was responsible, solely responsible, for the break. For this damage.

I reached out, lightly tracing my finger against some glass shards that remained in the metal frame, and I noticed that the thinner mullion *(or muntin?)* between the missing panes was bent and fractured at one end.

I'd done that.

The window was broken. Glass covered the floor. There would be consequences, and even in that not-quite-lucid-state I knew that I would accept them. I would pay for the repair. I would lose my membership. I would be arrested. Whatever it took. Whatever happened, I would accept the consequences. Because, finally, I was responsible. Solely responsible. Without question or ambiguity. And it made me laugh. A lightness spread with each gasping chuckle. A laughter that stopped as quickly as it had started.

Some time passed then, I think.

The next thing I remember was seeing a few bottles of tempera paint and a handful of brushes sitting on a table at the front of the room. They were leftover supplies from a paint night party earlier in the evening. An event where friends sipped wine and followed step-by-step instructions to create a sunset, a forest lake, a butterfly, or some other work of art. The kind of art that would be oohed and aahed over for a night and then stuffed in a closet or basement. The kind of event I'd been to more than once in that desert of time between art school and sketching Ed.

I laughed again at the sight of that paint. Standing with broken bourbon spilled at my feet, staring at cheap supplies for tipsy, would-be artists. Then I noticed the blend of colors—the deep blue and dusty green, the pale yellow, the glossy black—drawing me in.

It felt right as the blue smeared across the canvas, followed by the green. A wash of colors. Tiny flecks of red that I scarcely noticed were from the blood on my hands. Tiny cuts from the shattered glass. I layered the paint in thick daubs, then used a fine brush to etch in the details. Time began to stretch, to distort, the way it did when it felt right.

I watched a face emerge. Indistinct. The eyes uneven, the mouth crooked.

It was Liz. Or me. Or both of us.

It was beautiful. It was grotesque. And it felt like goodbye.

Day Twenty-Five

It's been twenty-five days since I went away.

Twenty-five days of living alone and going to therapy three times a week. Twenty-five days of drawing and painting, writing in search of my own story, and deciding the direction of my life. Twenty-five days of preparing for my first art show.

I didn't know where I would end up, the morning after I broke that window. I could have been headed to jail, but Karin chose not to press charges. I could have been headed to private, in-patient therapy, but my visit to Liz had scared me from that. It was clear I had to go somewhere. I had to get away. To get perspective.

It was Holly who suggested the month in Philadelphia, in a rented studio apartment where I could work in peace. It was George who agreed, after stipulating that I meet with a trauma therapist each and every week. It was Karin who pushed me to respond to Beatrice and agree to mounting a small show.

And it was me who did it.

George and I agreed it would be a trial run. A way to see if I'd be happier living in the city than I was in our quiet suburb. It didn't matter as much to him, he said, since his office was about halfway to Philly already. I couldn't entirely believe him, knowing how much he liked our suburban home and his network of nearby friends. To him, the city was a place to visit, not a place to live. But we found a furnished, short-term lease. George settled me in on day one, then left with a plan to visit on the weekends but otherwise give me space.

It was a gift. It was a risk. It was something I knew scared him to the bone. But it was something I needed to do. For me. For him. For everything. And he understood.

In the end, I was the one who started calling him nearly every night. I was the one who looked forward to every one of his texts and who had mailed him three postcards in the first week.

I've missed him every day. More so with each day, each week, that's passed. He's missed me, too, and it's nice to be missed. To reconnect with joy each weekend. To look forward to being back together, wherever we end up.

This isn't an ending I expected, but I'm grateful for what I've learned.

In twenty-five days, I've learned that I love the bustle of the city. I love its noise and energy. I love keeping my own hours, eating when I want, and sleeping when I want. I've learned that Beatrice inherited her father's heart and compassion, even if she didn't readily put those qualities on display.

I've learned to relax my art, to let go of the fine details and flow with my emotions, trusting that it will be better for the freedom.

The art for my small show is a curious mix. Portraits that are both classical and abstract. Some in finely shaded pencils. Others in fractured blocks of glossy paint. There's a painting of a blue toaster and a sketch of a young girl braiding flower stems into a wreath. There's sadness in my art. There's also hope and joy.

There are many things I miss about the suburbs. I miss my book club friends and my Art House friends. I miss my spacious house with its sunny deck and attached garage, and I miss my washer and dryer. I miss the spreading roots I'd overlooked. They may have been thin and neglected, but they'd also begun to grow and fill with potential.

What I haven't learned is any more of Liz's story. I don't know what happened in the short time between our visit and her death. Something had changed in her. During our visit, she had been eager, confident, nearly manic in her desperation to get free and start a new life. She'd been self-assured enough to make threats about blaming Ed's death on me. But she'd also been vulnerable, in telling me her story.

Maybe that vulnerability was too much for her. Or maybe my shock at those threats had called her bluff. Maybe she saw that it wouldn't be as easy as she'd hoped to plant doubt or pin it on me.

I've had other suspicions as well. Dark thoughts about why Sam was in that parking lot. I knew he hadn't visited

Liz that day. He'd tried but wasn't given access. Because Amy had turned him away. We'd assumed he'd followed me there and was waiting to talk to me again. But what if he were there to see someone else? What if he had another contact inside? A bigger plan?

Sam didn't want Liz to be set free. And, if he was right about his sister-in-law's meddling, Jodi might have had reason to worry about what Liz would say, too. Could Sam—or Jodi—have been more involved than anyone had realized? Was there a bigger, darker story?

I'd thought about contacting Amy, but I knew there was nothing more she could tell me. There was an ongoing investigation, and she'd already said I should let it go. That I should move on and focus on my own future. And she was right. Because, even if Ed's death had added a disturbing chapter, his story—and Liz's story—wasn't the defining story of my life. And if grown-up Mindy had questions, they wouldn't be for me. My part in that story was small and contained. My part was finished.

§

My art show opens tonight and there are six days left in our lease. Six days that George has already taken as vacation. Six days for us to explore my favorite places in the city together and decide whether we will find an apartment here or stay in the suburbs. Though that decision seems less crucial now. Traveling between both worlds, carving out a new path, a new life, is something I can continue to do. No matter where we live.

I'm not sure what I'll decide—what *we'll* decide—but I'm ready to discuss the options and make a decision.

For the first time in my life, something fundamental has changed.

I've always been to the left of life, letting my own journey be a series of reactions to other people's stories. But now I feel ready to make my own decisions, take charge instead of reacting. Take my own chances.

I'm done drifting.

I'm done giving weight to the imaginary voices in my head. I'm done being a witness, a side character, a ghost in the room.

I'm ready to stop hiding behind the storm.

Acknowledgments

Tapping into the emotion needed to create Megan took an enormous effort and has given *To the Left of Death* a special place in my heart. Many other challenges also showed up during the writing of this book, including two occasions of broken bones (once for my husband and once for me). Fortunately, I had the support of many close friends to see me through.

Though I mostly kept this manuscript to myself until I had a complete draft, special thanks go to my friend Jen Pool who read the first chapter when my confidence began to fail, then pushed me to keep writing (so she could keep reading!). Wendy McMullan and Angel Fischer also generously shared their time, and eagle eyes, to read the full draft, providing valuable feedback and encouragement.

Designing this book's cover was an experience of its own. My scenic designer son, Michael Cherry, helped translate my vague idea into a concrete vision. My artist friend, Kevin Bednarz, offered drawing tips that helped me get from concept to completed work, and suggestions from my artist/graphic designer friends, Rodney Roberts and Deanna Escobar, took my cover layout to a whole new level. Much love to you all!

Writing may be a solo effort, but community support is what fuels a large project when my energy lags and doubts creep in. Special thanks to Susan Shurtleff and Gretchen Schutte for listening and quelling my countless qualms. Thanks to Brian Palagyi for the laughter and online chats, to my yoga and comic shop communities for your local support, and to my neighborhood friends for your acceptance and love.

Again, I've left my husband for last, but in no way least. It would be impossible to list all the ways Peter continues to support me in my writing and in every aspect of my life. He put up with a lot of extra tears and turmoil through the writing of this book, so I'll try to make the next one a happier project!

To everyone who is reading this, thank you for reading, reviewing, and otherwise supporting my writing. As an indie author, simply getting my work into the hands of readers is a big challenge. Your support means the world to me!

Thoughts on Trauma

Writing a story in the first person presents certain difficulties, especially when your main character struggles with their mental health. *To the Left of Death* is the story of a woman who is living with the effects of trauma. Megan's experiences may feel familiar to some readers. However, like depression or anxiety, Post-traumatic Stress Disorder (PTSD) comes in many forms.

Some aspects of PTSD, such as dissociation and depersonalization, can be confusing and frightening to experience, yet they are not a sign of being "crazy." Millions of people live with these and other post-trauma symptoms while still maintaining normal, fulfilling lives.

While PTSD often affects war veterans, it can be a result of other trauma as well, including surviving assault, an accident, a natural disaster, or the death of a loved one. There is no specific type of trauma, or level of trauma, that leads to PTSD.

If symptoms of trauma are affecting your life, there are treatments that can help.

You can learn more about trauma through the PTDS Alliance (ptsdalliance.org) and the National Center for PTSD (ptsd.va.gov).

While Megan's struggle has a more hopeful ending, Liz's story gives us a glimpse into a deeply upsetting, yet sadly common crime.

Human trafficking happens around the world, even in suburban communities that are considered "safe." It affects countless victims, as trafficking is often misunderstood and under-reported.

If you suspect trafficking in your area, or want to learn more, visit the National Human Trafficking Hotline (humantraffickinghotline.org) or call 1-888-373-7888.

In the case of any trauma or mental health crisis, there is help available through the National Suicide Prevention Lifeline, online at suicidepreventionlifeline.org or by phone: 1-800-273-8255.

You are not alone.

About the Author

Susan Quilty is an indie author who has recently shifted her focus from selling freelance articles to publishing her own fiction. Her first novel, *The Insistence of Memory*, was released in 2017. She is currently working on multiple projects, including an adventure series for young adults. In addition to writing, Susan is a certified yoga teacher who has practiced yoga for over 10 years. You can learn more about Susan and her upcoming projects through social media and her website: SusanQuilty.com.

Discussion Questions

Note: Spoilers ahead.

1. In the opening chapter, Megan says she is not legally responsible for Ed's death. Do you think she is responsible in any way or is Liz solely to blame? Why might Megan feel responsible for Ed's death?

2. Megan describes herself as being "broken" and claims that she can sense "equally broken people." Do you think she has become adept at seeing other people's pain?

3. Part of Megan's healing involves reconnecting with Holly and making new friends at The Art House. What kept her from reaching out for so long? Do you think her friends could have tried harder to connect with her after Ed's death?

4. After arguing with George, Megan sketches Ed and has an imaginary conversation with him while she works. As their fantasy friendship grows, do you think talking to "Ed" in this way helps or hurts Megan?

5.   Megan hides her sketches from George, saying she wants to keep her art to herself. Do you think she had other reasons as well? Have you ever wanted to keep a hobby or interest to yourself?

6.   When fleeing to New York, Megan says she simply knew she had to go. Do you think she went to see Remy? Why do you think she let Becca join her?

7.   When the article about Megan and Ed goes viral, it both hurts Megan and helps her connect with Beatrice. Should the reporter have talked to Megan before writing about her? How might you feel if a traumatic event in your life was discussed in the national news?

8.   Both Sam and Liz share more information with Megan. Did either of their stories influence your beliefs about who was responsible for Ed's death? Do you agree with Megan's decision to let go of that day and move on with her own life?

9.   Megan's name is not given until her conversation with Detective Frye in "Day Twenty-One." Why might the author have waited so long to reveal her name? Why do you think it was revealed in this conversation?

10. Chapter titles are listed as days, and it is eventually explained that each chapter is a new day in Megan's journal. Did you have suspicions about where Megan was located while writing her story?

Also by Susan Quilty

The Insistence of Memory– Reality bends when Joanne discovers her husband's secret creation: a machine that can record memories and play them back in someone else's mind. Now Joanne must choose between continuing his project and protecting the privacy of her own dark past.

The Psychic Traveler Society Series – Fourteen-year-old Amanda Jones knows her life will change when she begins high school. She doesn't know that the old Victorian house in her recurring daydreams is about to lead her into worlds beyond her imagination.

This series, written for both young adult and adult readers, begins with *Healers and Thieves.*

Freely Written: A Podcast

Are you ready for a story break?

Join author Susan Quilty as she uses simple prompts to free write her way into strange, silly, or poignant tales. Weekly episodes offer new stories, while bonus episodes share behind-the-scenes commentary. Episodes are short, about 10 minutes each, and suggestions for future writing prompts are always welcome!

Find *Freely Written* on your favorite podcast app.

www.ingramcontent.com/pod-product-compliance
Lightning Source LLC
Chambersburg PA
CBHW061612190726
48288CB00007B/2290